In The Presence
OF
Knowing

By

Valarie Savage Kinney

In The Presence Of Knowing

In The Presence
Of
Knowing
Valarie Savage Kinney

Copyright © 2017

Book Design:

WICKED MUSE

Editor:

Leanore Elliott

DEDICATION

For my husband, John
I couldn't do this without you.
Everything I'm doing, I can only do because of you.

For my children,
Olivia, Savannah, Donovan, and Brennan
Keep chasing your dreams, always.

And

For all those who keep trying to force artists
To shave their square edges away
So they fit into the common, round holes
You probably won't like my books.

CHAPTER ONE

July 2010

Something was wrong with my baby.

I could feel this certainty within me, but when I tried to explain it to my doctor, he brushed it off as first-time mother jitters.

It wasn't.

Something was *wrong*. I would lie in bed at night with my hands resting on my swollen belly, feeling my baby kick inside me, and I knew that something was terribly, awfully wrong. But the tests had all come back showing my baby was healthy and strong, and I tried to make myself believe it.

My best friend, Layla, told me it was just a bad case of anxiety. After all I'd been through, she says, and it was true. The past several months had been some of the most difficult of my life. I left my boyfriend, Vince, after I found out I was pregnant. The baby was a surprise. His alcoholism wasn't. But the news of my pregnancy brought it all into focus for me. I stared at the two pink lines on that stick and felt something in my heart shift. For so many years, I had stayed faithfully by Vince's side as he tried and failed and tried and eventually quit trying to kick the bottle. And I loved Vince, I did. But he'd made his choices in life, and I couldn't stick around forever, waiting for him to wake up.

I always thought if I just held on long enough, loved him hard enough, showed him somebody believed in him, he would be able to quit. But he can't.

He won't.

Twice, he hit me. The first time, he was horrified at his actions and cried. Begged for my forgiveness. Promised to get himself into AA meetings again.

And he did, for a few weeks. Then he started missing meetings because he felt tired or because work had been rough that day.

The second time, he just stared at me lying on the floor.

I stayed flat on the ground, trembling. I could feel the heat of what would later become a bruise spreading across my face. Fear settled in my belly, real and true fear. I had never felt afraid of Vince before. *Stay still. Stay quiet. Don't make him mad. Don't move.* He stood there, furious, staring down at me with a look of utter and complete revulsion on his face. Like I was a nasty bug smashed on the bottom of his shoe and he couldn't wait to get rid of me.

"Next time, Keisha," he'd said.

Next time, what? I'd thought. Next time, it will be worse? Next time, he won't stop? I understood it in my bones for the threat it was meant to be, and I shook with terror.

Abruptly, he left. Stayed gone several hours and came home in the middle of the night. Passed out on the couch, like he couldn't stand to be in the bed with me.

The next day, he'd acted as though nothing had happened. No apology. No, "Baby, I'm sorry." But he wouldn't look me in the face for days. I guess he didn't want to see the ugly bruise that had appeared across my right cheek.

It was six days after the second time he hit me that I stood in the bathroom staring at those two pink lines. Something shifted in me, as the feelings of love and protectiveness I used to feel for Vince disappeared, as though a magician just snapped his fingers and yanked me out of a hypnotic state. Five years I'd been with Vince, and I had thought we would always be together. But those hopes changed. Had to.

Instead, those feelings transferred to my baby. I knew in a flash of time, I would do anything to protect this tiny little peanut growing inside me. With the knowledge that I was carrying a child,

I felt completely awash in love. Weak from the weight of it. Strong with courage.

The decision itself was easy. It was the aftermath of it that seemed hard.

Vince called or texted me thirty-plus times a day, begging for just one more chance. When he realized I wasn't coming back, he turned nasty, and I threw my cell phone in the trash, so I didn't have to deal with his angry communications any longer.

When I first left, I had no place to stay. My father had decided playing Daddy wasn't quite the thing for him when I was about three, and he hightailed it out of our lives. My mother is a homeless drug addict. She wasn't always like that. Somewhere along the way, the stress of being a single parent got to her, I guess. She started popping pills to help her stay awake while she worked two, sometimes three jobs. There were sporadic stints at community college that never lasted more than a semester, if that. By the time I was fifteen, she was addicted to cocaine. Off and on, I stayed with my grandmother, Mim, but the truth was, Mim was more than just a little bit off her rocker. Sure, I loved her and I still visited and made certain she had the things she needed, but I couldn't live with her. She wasn't stable. And besides, I worried Vince would hassle her if I was there.

I found myself knocking on Layla's door. Everything I owned I had stuffed in my tiny, rusted Ford Focus.

She opened the door, saw me with the bruise and the tears on my face, wrapped her arms around me and pulled me in, figuratively and literally. Into her house and into her life, weird as it was.

It was only a few weeks later when I turned into a fairy.

April 2010

Not a real fairy, obviously. That would be crazy, and I'm not crazy.

I used to work as a cashier at the kind of store where everything costs a dollar. It wasn't a bad job, not really. The pay kind of sucked but along with what Vince made at the factory, we did okay. The public tended to treat me like I was several leagues below them, and more than once I'd had something thrown at me. Balled up receipts, dented boxes. People in general are just angry, I think. More so than what they used to be. Or maybe I just noticed it more now because I had to deal with them so much at my job.

But my hours had slowly been getting cut, and my regular paychecks had dwindled to nearly nothing. Corporate had ordered management to take on more of our tasks and keep the rest of us below twenty-five hours a week. At just above minimum wage, that was barely enough to put gas in my tank. And besides, Vince would look for me there. Never been the type to pull a no call, no show, but a lot of things about me are changing. I didn't even call in to quit. Just stopped showing up. I imagine they got the hint. It would be a lie to say I didn't feel guilty about it, but once it was done, it wasn't like I could go back and change it.

Layla rented a little house in an area that was just on the brink of being a terrible neighborhood. It was mainly old timers who lived on her street. Lots of white-haired old ladies in flowered housedresses, looking at us with narrow, suspicious eyes from their porches. Layla had two bedrooms, but one was halfway converted into a work room. An old twin bed frame was shoved up against the far wall. A ton of boxes filled with yarn and sewing supplies were scattered all over the floor. Her sewing machine blocked half of one wall.

I stood staring at what was supposed to be my new home.

"I can move my work stuff into my room. At least, some of it." Layla sounded much more confident than I felt.

I did feel grateful don't get me wrong, but the room made me feel a bit claustrophobic. I'm tall as it is, broad-shouldered, wide-hipped, and about to have a belly the size of a mutant watermelon. My throat felt dry. I worked up a bit of spit in my mouth and swallowed hard. "Thanks, Lay," I said. My stomach wobbled. It'd been doing that a lot lately. "I appreciate you helping me."

"No problem, Keisha. It's going to be a good new start for you, I think. I know you weren't ready before, but this is the right move. Vince is a train wreck and he's just dragging you down with him."

I didn't tell her my news. I'd told her that I'd left Vince and quit my job. She could see the bruise on my face, plain as day. She knew that he'd hit me. It had been just over a week since his fist left that sweet little souvenir on my face. She'd known about his drinking for a couple of years, too. I used to try to hide it from her, but gave up after a while. There was only so much I could cover up, when Vince himself seemed proud of his habit.

I couldn't make the words come out. I turned to my friend and looked her hard in the eyes. She's shorter than I am so I had to look down. Her green eyes were watery as she stared back at me. I bent my knees and threw my arms around her, squeezing her in a tight bear hug. Then I covered my mouth and ran to the bathroom to throw up.

When I came out, Layla was digging through a plastic box, yanking out brightly colored skirts, puffy white shirts, and what looked like pirate corsets from bad Halloween costumes. Her super curly red hair looked frizzed out like she'd rubbed it with a balloon that was full of static. She squealed.

I braced myself.

Layla's squeals rarely signified anything good for me. Here's the thing about Layla: She's got a heart of gold but she gets these *ideas.*

Like when we were both twenty and she challenged me to see how many Walmart stores we could get kicked out of in one night.

It turned out to be six of them. Three of those six banned us for life.

Considering her idea at the time had been for both of us to dress up like clowns and then have me handcuff her to the cart while we ran through the stores shrieking, it's a wonder we didn't end up arrested.

Now she stood up fast, clutching a red satin corset with long black ribbons trailing off it. "Keisha, I've got an idea!" she shouted.

I was positive the idea would be a bad one. I flopped down on the couch. "An idea, huh? Tell me about it."

My life seemed to be completely upside down, and it was about to get a whole lot more strange.

I like to think of myself as a creative person. I crochet, and can do a lot with hot glue and glitter. But Layla took the notion of being creative to an entirely new level.

She sews. Technically, she's a seamstress. That was her day job. Summers, she worked at a Renaissance festival that was set on a few hundred acres of forest here in northern Illinois. Her business, On a Wing and a Prayer, started out slow and small but it turned out there's a real market for custom fairy wings. Who knew? She spent a lot of time taking in waists on skirts or putting hems in pant legs. The fairy wings, though, that's what she wants to do full time someday. Just travel from Ren faire to Ren faire, dressing like a slutty pirate and hawking her wings.

And apparently, she wants me to do this with her. Work as her assistant.

Evidently, I'm as nutty as she is, because I told her I'd do it.

But I'm not dressing as a pirate, wearing a short skirt and a boob-smashing corset. I may have made a lot of bad choices in my life, but I do have some standards.

That's how I ended up as a fairy.

I told her that I'd do it, and then I told her my other news. "Lay? I need to tell you something…"

I think she knew something big was up, because she just sat there quietly, waiting for me to go on, and Layla is not a quiet sort of person.

"I'm pregnant." Better to just get it out and over with, I thought.

It took a minute for the bombshell to sink in. She just sat there, blinking, her red curls springing out all over her head and making her look like a confused, modern Medusa. But then she started squealing and clapping her hands then talking about how we could make a tiny little dragon costume for the baby.

"Slow down, Lay. I'm not quite to the point I can think about dressing this kid up in cute costumes just yet." I leaned back against the couch. "I've got a lot to figure out still." I'm not generally the weepy type but I'll admit my eyes were a little damp right then. When I stopped to think about my situation, it was overwhelming.

"I'm sorry," she whispered. "Are you thinking about—about not keeping the baby?" She gripped my hands, holding tight. Her chin quivered.

I squeezed her hands in return. I already knew what I was going to do, but it meant a lot to me that she was giving me room to think about a different choice. "No. No, I'm definitely keeping it. It's just that thinking about having a child on my own, raising it on my own, that's scary. I'm homeless, unemployed, and single. It's a little bit terrifying, you know?"

Layla sighed, and stood up to begin walking in a circle around the living room rug. She ticked off numbers on her fingers as she paced. "Okay, listen. Number one, you are not homeless. You're welcome to stay here as long as you want to. I mean that… you know I mean it, don't you, Keisha?"

I nodded. "I know." And I do know it. I look around her tiny house and I am grateful. I wonder briefly where we will put a third person once the baby arrives, but I push the thought away. We can figure it out when the time comes. I'm lucky to have such a generous friend.

"Two, you are not jobless. I just gave you a job. It doesn't pay great, I'll grant you that much, but it's something you can do, and I think you'll enjoy it. And three, and I cannot stress this enough," she paused and looked at me so hard I felt like a naughty child, "you are *not* alone. You may not have a boyfriend, but you have a person willing to help you raise this child. I'm here, Keisha. I'm here and I love you and I will love this baby and help you forever."

Again, I'm not really the weepy sort, but sometimes I wish I were. Emotions are a hard thing for me to handle. I wish I had that release of tears other people seemed to embrace.

We worked together on clearing out the space that would become my bedroom – sooner or later – and she tried to talk me into calling the police about Vince.

I stubbornly refused. In the back of my mind, I knew I should have done it already. I didn't want to be questioned by the police. I didn't want to have my face examined by unfamiliar doctors. And I didn't hate Vince and want to ruin him. I just want him to be out of my life and I sure didn't want him to know I am having his baby. It seemed perfectly reasonable to me. Once the bruises healed, I felt certain I could just move on with my life.

I was wrong about that. Turned out, I was wrong about a lot of things.

It's never that easy for someone like me.

CHAPTER TWO

May 2010

The Renaissance festival ran from May to September. Early in the morning of the day it began, Layla presented me with the new costumes she had made for me. I tried and probably failed to muster the correct amount of enthusiasm in my facial features. It looked as though she had managed to collect all the tulle in the known universe, in every color imaginable, and made it into skirts for me.

I held the massive wads of flimsy fabric in my hands and made effort to produce a watery smile. "These are… great. Just great. Thanks, Lay."

She took the skirts from me and set several of them on the floor. Holding up one that was blindingly pink, she stretched the waist of it way out. "Look. See? The waists are all elastic so they can, um, expand as you grow."

"Wow. That's great. Really great." I could hear myself repeating the same word but felt unable to find a new one to use. "Great" was just about all I could think of to say. Visions of myself decked out in yards of tulle with a belly the size of Ohio filled my mind. I'd be a waddling, swaybacked fairy, and everyone else would stare and laugh at me. Oh, Lordy. What had I agreed to? I swallowed hard and found my throat was suddenly dry.

"Try it on! I'm sure they'll fit, but just to be certain. Then we'll have to get going to the fairgrounds to set up."

I took the offered mass of fabric and went to my teensy bedroom to change. I felt ridiculous, like a grown woman dressed in a child's costume.

Then when I opened the door and stepped out, Layla's face lit up like a Christmas tree. She clapped her hands and squealed at my appearance. "Look!" she cried. "Look at yourself in the mirror!"

I complied, turning toward the full-length mirror that hung on the wall between the bedrooms and the living room. The outfit I had chosen to try on was the one Layla called the Woodland Fairy outfit. My shirt was something like a silky brown tank top, with faux brown and green leaves sewn all over it. The skirt was lime green, reached to my knees, and was exceptionally full.

Layla ran up behind me and attached my wings, which were admittedly lovely, and had stretchy elastic bands that went around my shoulders to hold them on. The green and brown did sort of compliment my heavy black hair.

The only nice thing I could think of to say was, "It looks good with my hair."

"Oh, it does! It looks fantastic on you! Now I just need to do your makeup. Come out in the kitchen where the light is better so I can get you all done up."

I don't typically wear much makeup, but I let her do her thing. Least I could do, I guess. I sat quietly while Layla drew swirls on my face and eyelids with black eyeliner. Then she doused me with sparkly powder and pronounced me ready.

She disappeared into her own bedroom and came out ten minutes later in a long gold skirt, an off-the-shoulder white top, with a black corset. She held the corset against her chest and asked me to tie it in the back. I pulled the ribbons tight, but she demanded I pull them even tighter before I tied it. I obeyed but felt a bit guilty, because I felt like I was hurting her. When she turned around, her breasts were pushed up so high it looked as though they'd fall out if she sneezed. She said my cinching job was perfect.

In The Presence Of Knowing

Dawn had barely begun to crack when it came time for us to leave. We had filled Layla's van up with merchandise the night before, and hitched her little tin can camper to the back. We'd gotten rid of any perishable food, let the neighbors know we were leaving, then packed enough street clothes and costumes to last us. The little rusty camper looked old, but serviceable, and had a tiny refrigerator, which we planned to fill once we got to the grounds and were set up. I'd never been camping before, let alone considered living in an eight-foot-long camper for several months, but then again, I'd never considered dressing up as a fairy and appearing in public before either. After just a few weeks away from Vince, my life had changed so drastically I often couldn't believe it.

The festival took place two hours from Layla's house, in a small northern Illinois town called Windy Springs. I'd been nervous about Vince tracking me down since I left. He had never liked Layla – he thought she was weird and was jealous of the attention I paid her – so he hadn't bothered to learn where she lived. Knowing Vince, he was probably drunk out of his mind by now, still thinking I would change my mind and come back. Though he hadn't shown up to hassle me while I was at Layla's, now and again when I was in town, I had the feeling I was being watched. Like I had to keep checking over my shoulder for his old Buick.

Putting two hours' distance between us would make me a lot less jumpy, I hoped. The drive itself was pleasant enough, however, and left me feeling calmer than I'd been in weeks. I watched out my window as the sun rose and sat bright in the sky. Spring in the Midwest was a pretty time, and I enjoyed letting my mind wander a bit as we drove past the bright green trees and grass. Bright flowers were beginning to poke through the ground. I still felt ridiculous, but as though I had something to look forward to. I looked forward to the baby, of course, but that seemed so far away. I'd never been to a Renaissance festival before, and was more than a little nervous about what it would be like. But going with Layla made it seem like an adventure, and there was a little flutter of excitement in my belly.

As we whooshed through the city and made it onto the expressway, the little flutter turned to a terrible, wobbly feeling, and moved up to my throat. Realizing I was about to vomit, I tried to get Layla's attention by slapping at her arm.

"Ow! What're you doing, Keisha? Stop that!" she exclaimed.

The puke was hot in my throat and choking me, and I was afraid I wouldn't be able to hold it. Frantic, I covered my mouth with one hand and slapped harder at her arm and shoulder closest to me.

Finally, she glanced over, saw my brown eyes widened in panic, my hand over my mouth, and deduced correctly that I needed her to pull over.

As soon as she began slowing to a crawl on the side of the expressway, I leapt out and hurled enthusiastically.

She hurried around to my side and held my dark, frizzy hair back from my face, making soothing, nurturing noises as I tried to aim the trajectory of vomit away from the knee-length, suede boots she had lent me.

I could only imagine what passers-by were thinking about us as they drove past. A slutty pirate holding the hair of a lime green fairy who was puking her guts out, what a sight to behold!

By the time it was over, I felt too exhausted to wonder what others were thinking of us, too spent to even consider what the festival would be like. My only thoughts were focused on how much longer the sickness would go on, and how terrible the taste in my mouth was.

Layla unlocked the camper and came out a short time later with a box of baby wipes – she was a firm believer that anything in the world could be cleaned up with baby wipes – for me to clean my face off with and a pillow.

I thanked her and curled up in my seat with the pillow against the window, and closed my eyes. For a second, I was worried the motion of the vehicle would set the queasiness off again, but thankfully it didn't. I wondered if I could use a baby wipe to clean off my tongue. Soon enough, my exhausted body whisked me off to sleep.

When I woke, we were pulling into a grassy lot in front of a massive forest. Near the center, where there was a break in the trees, sat an enormous plywood cutout of a castle entrance. Across the top of the entrance, the words "Windy Springs Renaissance Festival" were emblazoned in thick cursive letters. We bumped along for a while, passing the lot Layla said was for patrons, until we turned a corner around the side of the forest. Here was what appeared to be a tent city, with bright cloths strewn over various tents and as I sat up and peered down a little farther, saw there were several small campers like ours already parked, as well as a few large, fancy RVs.

"Hey! You're up!" Layla said cheerily. "We're running a little late due to, um, having to make that stop earlier, so we'll have to hustle to get the shop set up on time. Usually, I come the day before to set up, but I wanted to finish your costumes before we came out, so we'll just have to move as fast as we can. Maybe I can find someone to help."

I felt immediately guilty. "I'm sorry I've put you behind, Lay. I feel bad."

She waved a dismissive hand at me as she slowed down, pulling our camper in next to a mid-sized black travel trailer with a pirate flag proudly waving from the front corner. "Oh, stop. It's fine. It shouldn't take us too much time. As long as my shop is ready to go when the gates open, we can take an hour or so to put on the finishing touches."

I blinked as tents waved open and a myriad of fairytale creatures began climbing out, moving toward the forest. Gnomes with pointy red hats, princesses, trolls, and a plethora of other fairies crossed the lot and disappeared into the woods. It made me feel a bit better to know I wasn't the only idiot dressed in yards of tulle. I also felt mildly disoriented, as though I'd fallen through a rabbit hole and was about to meet a queen fond of chopping off the heads of those who displeased her.

As if summoned by my sea of confused thoughts, a woman in an elaborate gold gown and sparkly crown stalked past us.

Layla immediately smacked me and bent down at the waist.

Staring hard at the back of her head, I whispered, "What are you doing?"

"Bow!" she hissed.

"Huh?" I gazed around. Everyone was either bent or kneeling. Still confused, I followed suit.

Seconds passed, and she stood back up straight. So did I. Everyone else began moving around and going back to their previous activities, as though we hadn't all just weirdly knelt and froze in position en masse for no apparent reason.

A man decked out in serious pirate gear stepped out of the door of the black trailer.

Layla smiled at him, lifting her hand in a half wave. She started toward him.

I grabbed her elbow and squeezed. "Hang on. What just happened here? Why were we all kneeling?"

She stared at me as though I was the one who had lost my marbles. "The queen was passing," she said, like it was the most normal thing in the world.

I paused a beat. "She's not a real queen, though… right?"

Layla raised her brows at me. "Here, in this forest, she is. If she walks past you, bow. Kneel. Get in the habit of it."

Bizarre didn't begin to cover this situation. Still, I nodded like I understood.

"Jack!" Layla cried, and lifted her long skirts to run toward him.

I followed at a much slower pace. My stomach was doing flip-flops again, and I held one hand against my belly in hopes it would somehow settle.

I watched as she enveloped the pirate in a tight hug, which went on longer than what it seemed it should for a couple of platonic friends. He murmured something in her ear, and she flushed dark red.

Standing awkwardly nearby, I didn't know what to do. I coughed.

Layla looked up at me and pulled back from Pirate Jack's embrace. She giggled and pushed red curls from her face. "Keisha, this is my friend, Dread Pirate Jack. He'll be around quite a lot. Jack, this Keisha. She'll be my assistant this summer."

The pirate pulled off his tricorn, crossed his arm in front of his abdomen, and bent forward. "Delighted to meet you, m'lady," he said in a deep and atrocious faux British accent.

I curtsied, though I can't say exactly why I did it. It just seemed to fit the occasion. When I rose, I looked up to find Mr. Dread Pirate staring thoughtfully at me, his admittedly beautiful blue eyes boring holes into mine. I paused for a moment and then turned toward my friend.

Layla cleared her throat, the Dread Pirate turned his attention to her, and the awkward spell was broken.

"We should get the shop set up, Keisha. Want to help me with these boxes?" Layla asked.

I felt suddenly energized, ready to take on the world. "Sure! Let's do this!"

The Dread Pirate had disappeared, into his trailer or into the forest, I supposed, and Layla pulled a collapsible wagon from the camper and set it up. We worked together, balancing boxes and bags in the wagon until it was loaded so high we were sure it would tip over.

"This way," Layla urged, and pulled the wagon toward the forest.

I followed, my shoulders laden with more bags, and we stepped through the back entrance to the festival. The trees formed a magical shelter from the harsh outside world, and as we walked the winding dirt path, Layla called out greetings to old friends. I felt a deep sense of peace and satisfaction, along with a slightly disoriented sensation. I had to admit, I was excited for this change of scenery.

A new chance. A new life.

…A fairy life.

CHAPTER THREE

A low-hanging tree branch caught one of my wings. I stopped and tried swatting at it. It didn't budge. Great. It would be just my luck to get caught in a tree, wreck the wings Layla had made for me, and make myself look like a total idiot in front of any potential friends.

"Layla! Lay!" I cried, but she was ahead of me, engaged in conversation with a couple of belly dancers, our mountain of stuff teetering precariously in the wagon. I stopped writhing for a second, took a deep breath, and tried to slowly free myself from the branch while attempting to maintain some semblance of dignity.

I pushed the shoulder that was under attack up toward the branch, and then pulled it down fast. The tree rustled, the branch came down lower, and somehow managed to insert itself deeper into my ornate bronze wing. This unfortunate turn of events left me with my right shoulder hunched up, my arm dangling, and the weight of the multitude of bags hanging from my shoulder became suddenly heavier. My right arm began to tremble from the pressure. I felt stupid and alone in this massive forest. The only person I knew was far down the path, too far for her to hear me if I yelled for help. I blinked hard.

Stupid, stupid, stupid. The little sprout of hope and peace I'd felt just a short time ago was gone.

Maybe if I stood still enough, nobody would notice me and eventually, Layla would come back for another load of boxes. Unless she took some other path back to the parking lot. Oh, Lord.

What if she never came to find me? What if I was stuck here for hours?

Despite my best efforts, everything in my life was turning out to be phenomenally stupid.

"Might I be of help, lash?" A male voice appeared out of seemingly nowhere.

Lash? I mentally ran through a list of things I might get called at this bizarre festival, dressed as I was. *Fairy, fae, wench, m'lady, madame...*

But "lash" wasn't something I could make any sense of.

A troll appeared before me. At least, I supposed he was a troll. He stood approximately five feet tall, with messy brown hair that hung down on his forehead and over his ears, with a bit of curl to it. His eyes were huge and green, with long, girlish lashes. Flat nose, and a remarkably wide mouth. And his teeth! A horrendous underbite left sharp, yellowed teeth poking up over his top lip. He was filthy, covered in mud, and was barefoot. He bent quickly at the waist and twirled his wrist.

"Gibble the Troll, at your shervishe, m'lady," he announced in a surprisingly deep voice.

I'm not sure why, but it seemed to me that a man – or troll – of his stature would have a high-pitched, squeaky little voice, which I guess spoke a little of my own prejudices. I felt heat rise in my cheeks. "Hi... um, Gibble. I'm Keisha." My arm was going numb. Hot pins and needles shot down to my wrist. Still, I managed some semblance of a smile. Part of the branch was now stabbing me between my shoulder blades.

"Ah, a new fae friend!" He grinned at me, which, with the underbite, was a gruesome expression.

Fae, Layla had coached me, was another word for fairy. I felt like part of the cool club, recognizing the language. "I could use some help getting loose from this tree, if you wouldn't mind, Gibble. It's beginning to really hurt."

"Sure thing, lash." He slipped around behind me his hands moving, pressing against my back, pushing my wing, wiggling the branch. He grunted. "Hold on a minute, dear. I can't quite reach it." Gibble took a few steps off the path and into the woods, found a large rock, and scooped it up. He seemed to be strong for such a small guy. Beneath the short, tattered sleeves of his muddy tunic-style shirt, biceps rippled.

I was reminded again that I shouldn't make assumptions about people.

Gibble hefted the big rock and carried it back to where I stood being harassed by a damn tree.

The wind blew. Leaves tickled my face. I sneezed. The force of the sneeze sent a sharp pain through my shoulder blade. "Ouch!" I cried.

"It hurting very much?" Gibble dropped the rock, moved it around until it seemed steady enough, and balanced himself on it.

I could feel him taking hold of the thick branch, working to release me of its grip. "I think I pulled a muscle in my shoulder. It hurts quite a lot, to be honest."

"Well, not to worry, dear. I've about got it. And... there we go!"

Immediately, the rush of release was all I felt. The agony in my shoulder blade lessened. I stumbled backward, my bags slid off my shoulder.

Gibble lost his balance. In what appeared to be a carefully planned and executed slow motion acrobatic move, he gracefully glided forward, tossed his arms out to the sides, and slammed into me.

I hit the ground, my back jamming into something hard in the path – a small rock, maybe – and it knocked the wind out of me.

Gibble landed on top of me, his face squarely cushioned between my breasts, his hands on my shoulders, and his legs between mine.

At first, I was too stunned to move and the pain in my back left me unable to draw enough breath to speak.

Thankfully, Gibble made the first move. He rolled off me and hurriedly stood, offering his hand to help pull me up.

Upright, I found myself unable to meet his eyes. The level of awkwardness was astounding. I twisted the toe of my boot into the dirt.

"Well then. You're free of the angry tree," he said, grinning, his underbite shining against the muddy skin around his mouth.

I laughed at his little rhyme, and felt much more at ease. I rolled my shoulders and arched my back. "Thank you, Gibble."

He waved his hand and replied, "No trouble." Circling me, he dutifully checked my wings for damage.

"Anything broken?"

"Nah. Looking fine, lash." He rounded my other side and offered his elbow. With his free arm, he hoisted my bags onto his shoulder.

I had to bend down a bit to hook my arm in his, but I did it anyway.

"And where are we headed with our fine bounty, Keisha?"

"My friend Layla's shop. On a Wing and a Prayer. Do you know where that is?"

"Indeed. Follow me, m'lady."

Down a winding path, through what was apparently some sort of medieval food court, over a small wooden bridge and another short dirt path we strode. Eventually, we arrived at a little wooden hut, where Layla was frantically setting out her creations on patchwork-cloth covered tables.

"*There* you are," she cried at our approach. "I wondered where you had gotten off to." She nodded at my new troll friend. "Good morrow, Gibble."

Gibble dipped his head and returned the greeting, "Good morrow, m'lady."

When her gaze returned to me, she screwed up her face and sighed heavily. "Just what were you off doing, Keisha? Your hair and makeup are a hot mess. Is that a... stick in your hair?" In one swift move, she was next to me, picking something out of my hair. Tossed the offending piece of wood off the path and into the forest. Then shook her head. "I'll have to fix your makeup and try to get your hair back into place before the gates open. I know you're new to this, but you really have to try to act the part."

"Sorry," I said, feeling instantly guilty. "I had a run in with, um, an angry tree branch."

Layla raised her brows and made a harrumphing sound. "Well, it looks like you survived it. Brush the dirt off your costume, anyway. We've got at least one more load to haul in from the lot, and the gates open soon. Let's go."

I waved to Gibble as we walked away. He seemed like a nice enough guy. At least I had made one friend in fairyland.

CHAPTER FOUR

I sat inside the hut while Layla wiped roughly at my face with a fistful of baby wipes. I had apologized repeatedly already. Logically, I recognized that the sense of instantaneous guilt was a leftover from my toxic relationship with Vince, but was unsure how to make the feeling stop. I blurted the same words out once more, "I'm sorry, Lay."

"Stop apologizing. It's all right. It was an accident."

"I know, I just … " I trailed off, unsure. "I appreciate you giving me a place to stay, and this job, and everything." I blubbered on. "I'm so thankful, and you're just the best, best friend I could ask for."

"Keisha. Shut. Up."

"I'm sorry."

Layla stood back and pinched her nose, squinted her eyes, and took a deep breath. "All right. It's all off, and now I need you to quit talking and just let me get your makeup back on." She picked up her basket of makeup and stepped toward me.

I opened my mouth once more, thought better of it, and clamped my lips shut.

"Good girl."

I focused on the feeling of her hands on my face, deftly brushing colors on my eyes, cheeks, and lips. I sat just experiencing the sensation of the sparkly black eyeliner swirling out around the corners of my eyes.

When my face was once again worthy of being a fairy, she turned her attention to my hair, patting it, twisting little pieces back to their places. "There!" she proclaimed. "You look great! Now, just help me hang these last few sets of wings on the rack, and we are ready for opening day."

As I stepped out of the darkened hut and gazed around, I was stunned to see the changes made around us in just those few minutes we had been inside.

Covers had been pulled down, doors thrown open, colorful decorations and signs set out. The lanes were filled with the cast in magnificent outfits. Down the lane, harp music wafted through the air. A jester in purple and orange stripes did flips down the path in front of us. In the air, a rainbow of butterflies flitted past.

Fairyland.

I blinked. Twice. Three times.

"Keisha? A little help, here?"

Startled, I turned from my reverie and picked up two sets of wings to hang up. A sound like an old church bell rang out, so loud I felt the reverberation of it in my bones, and my hand trembled a bit. For a brief second, it made me think of a warning of disaster. Like a tornado siren. "What's that?" I asked. "Is something wrong?"

"The bell? Oh, it's fine. It's just signaling the opening of the gates. It's go time!" She grinned broadly, totally at ease in her element.

Not for the first time, I wished I possessed her easygoing nature.

Peering down the lane, I saw the throngs of people pouring in. My heart picked up its pace. I wanted so badly to do a good job for my friend, but I worried about my ability.

My time as a cashier at the dollar store helped a lot, and I found after a few hours, it wasn't so different. Yes, I was dressed as a lime green fairy, and yes, my best friend was dressed as a slutty pirate, and yes, I was hawking brass wings to people dressed in bizarre medieval attire, but beyond that, it wasn't terrible. I didn't have a cash register to help me make change, but my brain must have picked up more than I realized at my old job, because the numbers seemed to come to mind almost automatically.

So many people came to Layla's shop, there was rarely a moment to sit down. Finally, around two in the afternoon, we had a lull in customers.

Layla grabbed a twenty-dollar bill from the pouch hanging from her belt and shoved it into my hand. "Go grab us some lunch. I want a chili bowl. Get whatever you want. We'll have to eat quick before traffic picks up again."

Dutifully, I started off in the direction of the food court, taking care to avoid any outstretched tree branches. Along the way, I noted the variety of shops. Handmade soaps, crocheted jester and gnome hats, chainmail. No two shops were the same, and I longed to browse through them at some point. A wave of dizziness whooshed through me and I stopped, breathing slow and deep. Probably a bit of dehydration. Food and drink was a good idea. I walked into the sea of competing smells that was the food court. Noisy was one way to describe it. Miasma of utter chaos was another. So many people.

Inadvertently, I crossed my arms in front of my stomach as I sought out the place that sold chili bowls, squinting into the sea of buildings and tables. My eyes landed on a towering building with an open upstairs window, from which a woman with a long blond braid was singing something in another language. Her voice was magical. The sign on the front of the building read, "Soup and a Song," and I figured that one was my best bet. I stood in line, letting my mind wander a bit, listening to the woman singing. The twenty was getting sweaty in my hand.

Finally, it was my turn, and I walked slowly back to On a Wing and a Prayer, balancing the two bowls heaping with chili cautiously in my hands. The bread remained surprisingly cool, despite the bubbling brew inside. It smelled weirdly good to me, and I wondered at the bizarreness of vomiting up things as plain as dry cereal or toast but craving spicy foods such as this. Pregnancy, overall, was a strange thing.

As we hunched over our meal, Layla offered bits of gossip and introductions to cast and regular vendors who walked past us.

Two men dressed as gnomes with pointy red hats stopped to say hello, and Layla told me their names were Grok and Bork. I repeated their names in my head, so I wouldn't forget. They seemed friendly enough, both with blond hair and pleasant smiles.

Gibble stopped by to visit for a few short minutes. I learned the name of the queen was Natasha, and that she was as haughty outside the festival as she was when in character.

Juniper, a round, jolly woman who made her own soaps and lotions, breezed by to introduce herself. Juniper's long silver hair was wound round her head in a glorious crown of a braid. Her long green tunic seemed perfectly suited to her kind, sweet nature.

Soon enough, the traffic had picked up again, and we were back on our feet, busy for hours.

The rush slowed to a trickle during the final hour of the day, and I realized how much my feet and back ached. I had been surprised at how many people were so invested in coming to this faire.

"Is it always this busy?" I asked Layla, as we rearranged some of the racks and items to cover the bare spots. There was plenty more merchandise, but it was out in the camper still, and she said it wouldn't be worth it to restock the shop when the faire was getting ready to close. We would start all over again tomorrow.

"No. Usually opening weekend is one of the busiest of the season. Pirate weekend in June is fairly busy, and by September, we get a lot slower. But we are usually steady enough to do decent business."

"And through the week when it's closed, what do we do?" I imagined long, lazy days, waiting for the weekend. Much like an extended, lackadaisical camping trip.

"We will be busy then, as well. I've got a good stash of merchandise, but that will start to run out by next month or so. When the festival is closed, I will teach you how I make the wings and a few other things, and you can start helping me get some inventory going. We'll go into town for supplies when we need them, and to do our laundry."

Inwardly, I sighed. So much for the relaxing camping vacation. Another thought popped into my head. "I have a doctor appointment in two weeks. Do you mind if I use the van to go? I'm not sure how often I'll need to go to appointments." I smiled apologetically.

"That's fine. I can go with you if you want. If you feel better having some support."

It was true that I needed some kind of support system, and Layla was about all I had. I hadn't yet told Mim. My mother was unreachable as far as I knew. I could leave Layla's cell number at Mim's place. Maybe Mom would drop in some time. When I went back to town for my doctor appointment, I decided I would swing by Mim's and fill her in on the news of my impending bundle of joy.

I rubbed at the muscle spasm in my lower back. The guests – or patrons, as Layla called them – were finishing up the last of their shopping and heading toward the gates. The sun was getting lower in the sky and the temperature was cooling off. I helped Layla take her merchandise down and set it in our little hut inside plastic totes. We had been so busy through the day that the hours had passed quickly, but now fatigue washed over me. I plopped abruptly down on one of the wooden stools that sat outside the shop for patrons to rest on.

"You okay?" Layla asked, concern evident in her green eyes.

"Tired, is all. And I could probably use something to eat. Are we just on our own for dinner, then?" I asked, secretly hoping we could just order a pizza somewhere and eat in the camper.

"There's a potluck supper every night of faire, should be ready in an hour or so. The rest of the week we'll make our own."

"Oh." I pushed my shoulder blades together as hard as I could, then released them. Rolled my neck backward. Hunched my shoulders up and down. My muscles felt a little looser. "Can we change? Or do we have to keep the costumes on?"

Layla laughed. "Nah. We can change now. Go ahead back to the camper and put on something comfortable. I'll meet you there in a few."

Relieved, I wandered back the way I had come in that morning, carefully avoiding the offending tree branch. By the time I made it back to the camper, the sky was filled with such vibrant colors, I stopped and stared for a moment.

Dread Pirate Jack passed by me, offering a genial wave in my direction.

I raised my hand in return. Once inside the camper, I pulled sweats and a baggy t-shirt from my suitcase and shoved some boxes out of the way so I could have a little more space to change. I should have waited for Layla before I started trying to get out of my getup, but I was so uncomfortable the thought of waiting even ten more minutes seemed far too much. I slipped off my boots, got the wings off after a few difficult tries, and slid the shirt up over my head. A wave of dizziness came over me and I sat down on the tiny camper sofa. I was overly tired and had waited too long to eat, a habit that hadn't caused me problems before, but coupled with a pregnancy, it was catching up to me. I tipped my head back and closed my eyes for a second.

"Keisha? Keisha!" Layla was up in my face, shaking my shoulder.

I launched upright and immediately got so dizzy I had to sit back down. I rubbed my hand across my eyes and moaned. "What? What's going on?"

"You fell asleep. Are you sure you're all right? Did I overwork you today?" One red curl bounced merrily in front of her right eye.

My brain was working to get more awake and I sat there, blinking hard. "I must've konked out when I came in to change." *When I came in to change. Oh Lord.* I hadn't changed, had I? Looking down, I noted my sadly sparse attire of the green tulle skirt and a strapless bra. At least I hadn't removed my bra before I dozed off.

"She okay?" a male voice called through the tiny metal door.

"Yeah! Fine!" Layla yelled back.

"Who is that?" I whispered.

"Jack," she replied, and a silly little smile spread across her face.

I scrambled to pull a blanket over my exposed top half, and hissed, "Don't let him come in here!"

Layla laughed. "Be out in a second, Jack!" To me, she asked, "Are you going to come and eat with the rest of us, or do you want me to just bring you a plate, so you can rest?"

I weighed my options. I could change, go sit with a bunch of people I didn't know and eat a decent meal. Or I could stay holed up in the camper, rest until Layla came back with food for me, and eat in peace and quiet.

The notion of peace and quiet won out. "I'll stay here, if you don't mind, Lay. I'm so tired."

"No worries. I'll be back after a bit with your food."

The thin door clanked shut, and I could hear their voices trailing away.

I changed into my sweatpants and a t-shirt then curled up on the couch that would be my bed for the run of the faire. It was upholstered in a scratchy, orange and brown plaid fabric but felt heavenly as I settled down with a pillow and blanket.

Later that night, I woke with a horrifying sense of dread filling me. I felt panicked, as though I had just had a terrible dream. Sweat and chills warred for the dominant sensation. Heaviness in my chest left me struggling for a deep breath.

That was the first time I knew something wasn't right with the baby. I cupped my palms against my still-flat belly and wished for my baby to be safe. I begged a God I wasn't sure I believed in to change the knowledge that had settled within me.

In desperate need of the touch of another human, I grabbed the corner of my blanket, draped it around me, and stumbled into Layla's bed, which folded down from the table and benches it was during the daytime. It was extraordinarily uncomfortable, but I curled up next to her warm body and tried to take up as little space as possible. I stared into the darkness and worried, my mind an endless carousel of terrifying possibilities.

When morning came, Layla opened her eyes, stared at my face, and promptly screamed.

I must've looked worse than I thought.

"You're sure you're okay?" Layla asked me for the umpteenth time.

"I'm fine. It was just a nightmare or something, I think."

She looked at me hard, as though she knew I was lying. She was right. I was. But any logical way to express how I felt was lost to me, and regardless how many ways I tried to spin it, saying I woke from a dead sleep certain something was wrong with my baby made me sound like an idiot.

I couldn't explain it, not even to myself, really. It was just something I knew, the same way I knew if I peered into a mirror, my eyes would be brown and my hair would be a mess of dark, frizzy kinks. I tried to fill my mind with other thoughts as I readied myself for the day, but the dread settled into my belly like a weight.

"All right." She gave me a look that said it wasn't all right at all, and she'd be bringing it up again, sometime. "Today won't be as difficult as yesterday. We'll just have to get the merchandise out on the racks and tables. We'll probably be just as busy, though."

I shimmied into my hot pink tutu and pulled on my boots. "Did I do okay yesterday? And can you help me with the wings?" I handed them to her and stood quietly as she fastened them securely to the back of my outfit.

Finishing her task, Layla grasped my shoulders and spun me toward her. She narrowed her eyes and started in on my hair, twisting, tucking, pinning it into submission. "You did fine. If you think you can, you should try to start getting into some sort of accent. Listen to the cast and other vendors, and copy that. It doesn't need to be perfect, just try to get into the spirit of it. Aim for something vaguely British." She smiled in a way that was meant to be encouraging. "We'll put a case of water in the wagon and take it back to the shop for you today. I don't want you getting dehydrated."

I smiled back for three reasons. I wanted my friend to be happy. I didn't want her to worry about me. And because I hoped that if I faked happiness long enough, I would start to believe it myself. "Sure," I replied, and thought back to the way I'd heard most of the cast speak the day before. I had been so busy learning the ropes at the shop that I hadn't paid much attention, other than when I had spoken with Gibble. Oh, Gibble! I hoped to talk with him again today, if the opportunity arose. He seemed like a nice, funny little guy, and a potentially good friend. "I hope Gibble stops by today. He seems nice."

"He is. He's had a rough life, but his struggles have only made him kinder. You couldn't meet a sweeter man, really."

Intrigued, I asked, "Is that so? What happened to him?"

"Not my story to tell, Keisha. But Gibble's pretty open about it. Give him time, I'm sure he'll open up to you." She hefted a case of water onto her hip, and opened the camper door.

I followed her once again into the forest, hoping all the while, the sense of unease would disappear.

And that no angry tree would attack me today.

CHAPTER FIVE

Halfway through our second day, I felt like I was really getting into the groove of the whole thing. I kept remembering to do my admittedly bad accent at least half the time, and though I got a few odd looks from customers, it really did make the job more fun. I watched the way some of the other vendors and cast would banter playfully back and forth, and quietly wished I could let loose and join in.

Dread Pirate Jack stopped by several times during lulls to visit with Layla. At one point, she asked him into the hut to help her locate something, and I had a sneaking suspicion something else was going on.

Gibble passed at a fast pace, clearly on the hunt for someone.

I raised my hand in greeting, but he walked right past without even a hint of recognition. I tried not to let myself feel hurt. Other than Layla, Gibble had been the only other person I'd talked to at any length in this bizarre forest, and I had hoped to strike up a friendship with him.

A few minutes later, he passed by again. This time, he stopped. "Lash," he began, "might ye have noted our Dread Pirate around anywhere?" His eyebrows – beneath their smear of mud – rose hopefully.

What an awkward predicament. I knew where he was – doing something in the hut with Layla, and I was darn sure they weren't in there trying to find a stray box of wings.

I wiggled my eyebrows at Gibble, and tipped my head toward the hut.

He raised his eyebrows in return.

I wiggled my brows again, this time with more enthusiasm, and dipped my head harder in the direction of the hut.

Two customers paused their perusal of wings and stared at me.

Gibble had an absurd, bewildered expression on his filthy face.

Apparently, I had some sort of deficit in my ability to communicate nonverbally. Giving up, I stooped down and leaned in toward the troll's ear – intending to whisper the Dread Pirate's whereabouts – but stopped when the door to the wooden hut banged open.

Layla walked out, patting her messy red hair back into place and smiling broadly at us. Her obnoxiously red lipstick was smeared up toward her nose and as she walked past me, I realized the big drawstring bow that belonged on the front of her skirt was merrily protruding from the center of her lower back.

Jack slipped quietly out the door, then sidled over to the side of the hut and out onto the path, where he melted easily into a crowd of costumed cast and patrons.

I pointed toward him, and Gibble followed my gaze. He grinned and winked at me, taking off in the direction the wayward pirate had gone.

"Layla," I whispered, slinking up alongside her as she showed off one of her creations to a patron, "you've got a little something on your face."

"What?" She turned toward me, blinking.

I rubbed the space between my upper lip and nose and gave her a significant look.

She just shook her head in confusion.

I gave up trying for subtlety. "You have lipstick smeared all over and your skirt is on backwards," I said in a normal tone of voice.

The woman who'd been considering a set of wings turned her head away abruptly, but still, I heard her when she giggled.

Layla blushed and widened her eyes, lifting her skirt and ducking back inside the hut with a little squeal.

Finishing the transaction with the customer, I wrapped her wings carefully in paper and slid them into a bag that had 'On a Wing and a Prayer' printed in calligraphy across the center. Handing them over, I decided to embrace the atmosphere of the faire and said cheerfully, "G'day, lash!"

"Um, sure," she replied vaguely and wandered across the way to watch a belly dancing show.

Layla stepped daintily out of the hut, her makeup perfected and her skirt once again forward-facing. Either she had applied more blush to her cheeks or the deep rose hue was an indicator of embarrassment. "Do I look okay?"

I eyed her up and down. "You look perfect. I promise." Grabbing a bottle of water from beneath one of the tables – the long tablecloths hid them nicely – I unscrewed the top and took a long sip. "So, you and Jack, huh? How long has that been going on?" I was only mildly miffed. I had been hoping for years Layla would find somebody who would treat her right, so the fact that she hadn't told me she had a hot pirate boyfriend left me feeling a little bit betrayed. But more than that, I was happy because she seemed happy.

Her eyes dodged mine. "Oh, it's not really official or anything, you know. We hung out a lot last year during the season, and we've been texting off and on since then." She pulled a couple of baby wipes out of their container and set about cleaning a nonexistent smudge on the hut door.

"Is there some reason you've been keeping it quiet?" An awful thought struck me. "He's not, like, married or anything, is he?" The second the words were out of my mouth, I was ashamed for even thinking them. Layla was an honest person. Cheating wasn't something she'd be into doing.

She paused her nervous cleaning, clutching a wad of baby wipes in her fist. "No, no. Nothing like that. We're both free, that way. It's just… we are taking it slow. He's been hurt before, and so have I. We aren't ready to jump into anything serious. Right now, it's just fun."

"I see." Layla had been through a series of unfortunate relationships that had ended badly. I could understand why she'd want to take it slow. I hoped this pirate guy could see what a wonderful, sweet person Layla was. Maybe I would have a talk with him, find out exactly what his intentions were. I shook my head. This becoming a parent thing was getting to me. Layla was a big girl, she didn't need me to be her mom. "I hope it works out for you, Lay. You deserve it."

She grinned back at me, and resumed scrubbing the door. "Me, too, Keisha. Me, too."

The day had become so warm, I felt persistently dried out. My tongue felt like sandpaper, and I was blowing through the bottled water so fast, I thought I might have to go back to our camper for another case. I dragged my forearm across my sweaty forehead and guzzled another bottle. As soon as the last few drops made it into my mouth, I realized the sudden rush of water wasn't settling well in my belly. It flipped. It flopped. And I felt certain I was about to hurl all over our merchandise. Frantically working to remember which direction held the nearest port-a-potty, I started left down the path, then made a quick right and stopped abruptly, clapping my hand over my mouth.

I wasn't going to make it.

Hot vomit leapt up my throat, and with no other option but to stand in the lane puking in front of the patrons, I ran into the forest. Hoping the twenty feet or so I'd made it in would be far enough away from the faire activities to afford me some privacy, I held the trunk of an elderly birch tree and bent over, emptying my stomach into the dirt and grass. It seemed to drag on for hours while my stomach muscles began to tremble and ache with effort.

At some point, I felt a sturdy hand resting on my lower back and took a modicum of comfort in knowing I was no longer alone. Assuming Layla had witnessed my less than graceful departure from the shop and had come after me, I remained in position, one hand on the tree, one braced against my knee, heaving and desperately wondering how much longer this morning sickness would last.

When it was over, I closed my eyes, leaned back against the tree and slid down, snot dripping down from my nose and something suspiciously warm dribbling from my chin. I felt about as unattractive as humanly possible. I half-expected Layla to attack my face with a bunch of baby wipes and when that didn't happen, I opened my eyes to find my companion was not, after all, my best friend in all the world; instead, the wide-eyed, filthy face of a troll stared compassionately back at me.

"Hey, Gibble," I said. "I thought you were Layla." I should probably have felt embarrassed, but was far too exhausted for such frivolity. The muscles in my legs shook violently, and I drew my knees up toward my chest.

Kneeling before me, Gibble produced a surprisingly stark white handkerchief from the pocket of his mud-covered pants and offered it to me. I took it, wiping my face off the best I could and then settling back against the tree. The hot pink of my tulle skirt seemed even more ridiculous in this environment, and I managed a weak smile.

"Thank you," I told him. "I'll wash your handkerchief for you. Sorry." I wadded up the fabric square and set it in the dirt. "Gross, right?"

If I expected Gibble to be horrified at my disgusting appearance, I was mistaken. Tenderly, he brushed some random wisps of hair out of my face, quietly looking into my eyes. That was one terrible underbite, I thought again. Why hadn't his parents done something about it when he was a child? I hiccupped. The puddle of vomit was just about a foot away from us, and the smell, in the heat, was beyond unpleasant. I turned my head from the sight, but the scent of it remained unavoidable.

Gibble turned his body, so he was sitting next to me, and slipped his arm around my neck, drawing me in against his shoulder.

I barely knew him, but the gesture of kindness spoke volumes to me about his personality. I felt enormous next to his slight frame, but forced myself to relax against him. It had been a long time since anyone had touched me so tenderly, and it simply felt good. It felt *safe*.

"Poor girl. Heat got to you, eh?" he said, pressing his cheek against my head and tightening his hold around me.

The heat, the water, the fact that I'm pregnant and single and I think something is wrong with my baby...

"Something like that," I replied. "Thanks for helping me."

"Well," he said, "we all need a little help now and again, don't we? We can hang out here for a while, and when you feel you can, I'll walk you back to Layla. Good?"

"Sounds good, Gibble. Thanks, again."

As we sat there, my head on his shoulder, his arm around me, I thought again about how many different twists and turns my life had taken in such a short time.

My hot pink tulle skirt and long brown boots made an incongruous contrast to Gibble's muddy trousers and filthy bare feet. Both of us sat with our legs out straight, and his feet only reached to the middle of my calves.

The sun streamed in through the trees, and next to me on the grass, my unfortunate contribution to the forest glistened.

"I think you should try to eat something bland, like crackers," Layla suggested, as she pulled money from the cash box to buy our lunches. "Gibble told me you were really sick." Concern filled her eyes as she handed me the money.

I crinkled my nose. The thought of chewing dry crackers was distasteful, to say the least. "I was, but now I just want one of those chili bowls."

"You are stubborn as the day is long, Keisha. Whatever. Get what you're going to get, then. When you get back, I'll go find myself some food."

"You do realize I'm an adult, right? I can eat what I want without asking you for permission?"

She made a harrumphing sound. "Yeah, well, when you get sick, don't think I'll help you out again."

I stared her down. If I was sick again, she'd do what she could to help me out regardless of what I'd eaten, and we both knew it. I spun on my heel, which turned out to be a bad idea because I got terribly dizzy all at once, and flounced off.

I ordered my chili bowl at Soup and a Song, getting a kick out of listening to the girl in the tower singing as I waited. Though I could have sat down at a table to eat my lunch, I hurried back to On a Wing and Prayer to wolf my food down. The food court had so many competing smells it left me feeling overwhelmed and nauseated.

Watching Layla saunter off with Jack for her own break, I found myself smiling. My new surroundings were bizarre but I found I was developing a fondness for medieval music, and the belly dancing show that happened four times a day right across from us was always enjoyable. I also got a feeling that Gibble and I were developing a solid friendship. I was swaying slowly back and forth to the harp music wafting down the lane when the pain first struck me.

It felt hot and sharp, and shot through my abdomen like lightning. Caught off guard by such blinding agony, I crossed my arms over my stomach and dropped to my knees, crying out.

Voices surrounded me. Layla was speaking rapidly to someone in a low tone when I cracked my eyes open I could see that several security guards—they were the ones in matching plaid kilts and red berets, it was easy to pick them out—were forming a circle around me, standing straight with arms crossed, blocking me from the view of any gawking passersby.

Dread Pirate Jack knelt next to me and had one hand encircling my wrist. He was staring intently at his open pocket watch. He caught me looking and dropped my wrist, switching his focus instead to asking me questions. "Keisha? Can you tell me what happened?" He had dropped his accent, and long, beaded beard braids swayed from his chin. Black eyeliner surrounded his eyes, which were narrowed with concern.

"I had the most awful pain through my stomach. It was so sharp, I couldn't stay standing up. I think I blacked out."

He nodded, continuing with his interrogation, "Left side, right side? Throbbing pain? Have you been ill otherwise recently? Layla said you were sick earlier. Do you still have your appendix? Gall bladder?"

"Sharp, hot pain. Not on either side in particular, just all through my abdomen and lower back. I've never had any kind of surgery."

He placed his thumbs on my eyelids and pushed up, looking deeply into my eyes. "Any ongoing health concerns? Allergies?"

The baby. Something was wrong with the baby. I knew it, and I knew just as well that whatever was wrong wasn't something I could fix. My teeth began to chatter. I motioned for Jack to come closer.

He leaned down, his beard braids tickling my cheek. "What is it?" he whispered. His tricorn hat formed a barrier between us and the myriad group of onlookers.

I swallowed hard. "I'm pregnant," I whispered back.

Nodding, he asked, "How far along?"

Why I was giving my personal information to a pirate who was practically a stranger to me, I didn't know, but he seemed capable, and I desperately wanted someone who knew what they were doing to keep my baby safe.

"About eight weeks, I think. I haven't gone to the doctor yet. I had an appointment …" I trailed off. My first appointment was scheduled for two weeks from now. Would I even need it after today? A hard lump formed in my throat and my chin wobbled.

He helped me sit up, removed my fairy wings, then reached one surprisingly strong arm beneath my neck, and the other under my knees. Whatever he did in real life when he wasn't acting like a flamboyant pirate, it'd built him some solid muscles. He scooped me up and stood, and the crowd murmured.

"They're here," Layla said, and the group of kilted security guards surrounded Jack and I en masse as we headed toward the gates.

"Who's here?" I asked Jack, my head flopping against his chest as he walked. Security stomped along around us, and I felt like some Hollywood starlet, surrounded by my bodyguards.

"Ambulance. I'll go with you to the hospital, get you checked out."

We crossed through the front gates, and the sun was irritatingly bright. I shut my eyes against it. "What about Layla?" I asked. I didn't want to seem ungrateful, but the thought of Jack riding with me in the ambulance made me uncomfortable.

"She can't leave right now. I can."

I didn't understand why that was, but since I was being lowered onto a stretcher, and Jack was barking information and orders at the EMTs, I let it go for the moment.

The EMTs buckled me in and jostled me around a bit, as they loaded me into the back of the ambulance.

Jack climbed in behind me. He spoke rapidly to the female EMT who was placing an IV in my left arm.

I couldn't begin to keep up with their conversation. It was full of weird words I didn't understand. I closed my eyes and tried to think of happy, peaceful things. I imagined holding a fat, healthy baby in my arms. Dimples. Soft hair. Big eyes.

The ride to the hospital seemed longer than it probably was.

After he finished talking with the EMT, Jack turned his attention to me. "Hanging in there?" he asked, squeezing my hand.

We must have been on a dirt road, because I felt every bump and jolt. Though we were for all accounts and purposes strangers, Jack's presence was a surprising comfort. His hand felt warm and strong on mine. "I'm scared, Jack," I replied. "I don't want to lose this baby." The pain throughout my abdomen was fierce and I had to force myself to take deep breaths. My teeth – and, it seemed, everything else inside me – chattered hysterically.

"Hush, now, Keisha. We'll do all we can to stop that from happening. Try to rest. We're almost there."

The ambulance took a wide turn and slowed to a stop. The back doors of the rig swung open, and I was once again, at the mercy of the none-too-gentle attendants. Desperate fear struck me hard as I was lifted down and I wished Layla was with me. To be in such pain, at risk of losing my baby, and on top of that, alone at a strange hospital was just about more than I could bear. Panicked, I reached blindly outward, waving the arm that wasn't attached to an IV. "Jack?" I cried out, ashamed at how needy and weak I sounded. But the thought of being left alone in this unfamiliar place was almost worse than the pain that continued to torture me.

"I'm here, I'm right here," he assured me, suddenly appearing on my left. "I'm not going anywhere. Don't worry." He broke into a jog to keep pace with my entourage, and in a short span of time, I was in a triage room, hooked to multiple monitors, and waiting on a visit from a physician.

The doctor came, barked out several brief questions, and busied himself with reading the printouts from various machines that were attached, in one way or another, to me. "Any bleeding?" he asked, peering at me above a pair of black plastic bifocals.

"No." He looked tall and broad. He narrowed his eyes at me as though he expected the situation was my fault. He was clearly aware of his intimidating nature and used it to his professional advantage, which might have come in handy when demanding answers of drug addicts and the like, but only served to make me feel doubly frightened. I swallowed hard. My throat was so dry, but they wouldn't allow me anything to drink until they were certain what was going on.

The doctor grunted and continued to pepper me with questions, his tone laced with disapproval. I answered them the best I could, though I could hear my voice wavering as I did. Guilt washed over me, sticking to me like a heavy second skin. I had done something to cause this. It was my fault. It had to be.

Maybe I didn't deserve to be a mother, after all. Maybe the reason everything had gone south with Vince *was* because of me.

My own mother had abandoned me. Maybe terrible parenting was in my DNA. Despite her many failings, at least my mother had managed to get me born, however. It didn't seem as though I could manage that much.

Whatever it was I had done, I wouldn't do it again, if only we could fix it this time. The doctor's voice had become little more than a muffled drone as my brain shot into overdrive. Had I stood on my feet too long this weekend? Eaten something that could have harmed the baby? Unknowingly consumed caffeine or something else that was toxic in early pregnancy? I replayed the events of the last few days over and over in my mind. The smell of antiseptic hung heavy in the air, and only added to the lurching in my belly.

"Keisha? I'll be right back," Jack said, as he stood and strode across the tiny room. "A word with you, doc?" he asked, and motioned for the older man to follow him outside the curtain.

When Jack came back inside, he was alone.

"What did he say?" I wanted to know as much as I didn't. Once I knew for sure the baby was gone, I would never be able to erase the knowledge. I bunched the thin blanket in my fists.

He looked directly into my eyes and told me the baby appeared to be fine. He patted my shoulder awkwardly. "A nurse will be in to explain the test results to you in a few minutes in detail, but the important thing is that the baby looks like it's doing fine right now, okay?"

"Okay," I replied in a tiny voice, letting the information sink into my mind. I fought to calm my nerves, taking deep, slow breaths. "Okay, okay, okay."

Jack returned to his seat next to me. "Is there anyone you want me to call for you? Your, um, boyfriend or whatever?"

"No. There's nobody." My voice hitched, and I cleared my throat hard.

"Oh. Well, I'll just wait here with you until you're discharged, and then we'll call Layla and see when she can come pick us up, then, all right?"

"Okay." Beyond relief that my baby was safe, another thought had been tickling my brain for the last couple of hours. "Jack?"

"Yeah?"

"When we left the fairgrounds, you said you could leave, but Layla couldn't. Why was that?"

"Right, well, my dad owns the festival. He might have gotten mad if Layla left her shop unattended, but he won't do anything to me." He grinned at me, the particular smile of a really, *really* spoiled little boy.

"Ah, I see. And the reason you're spitting out medical jargon left and right, acting like you know everyone here is because… "

"Because when I'm not playing pirate, I'm a nurse here, in the NICU. And also because my mom happens to be the director of the hospital." Once again, he gave that little *I can do no wrong* grin.

The pain had subsided, other than some mild intermittent cramping, and I relaxed a bit. Now that the immediate threat seemed to have passed, I had time to consider how ridiculous the two of us must have looked – a fairy on the stretcher, a pirate running alongside her into the ER. A hysterical laugh escaped me. I clamped a hand over my mouth and felt red rushing to my cheeks.

Jack questioned me with a narrowing of his eyes.

"We must look ridiculous. I mean, at least I'm in a hospital gown now. You're... well, look at you."

Jack looked as though he had just come off a ship. In Hollywood. Long dark beard braids, equally dark and even longer dreadlocks, a bandanna with strings of beads dangling off it. Puffy white shirt, baggy brown pants, more gaudy rings than any one person should ever wear. He just laughed and waved a hand. "Not the first time they've seen me in garb, won't be the last, I'm sure."

He was a nice guy, I decided. A little arrogant, to be sure, but good at heart, and I hoped he and Layla worked out.

At least he hadn't left me alone to deal with this crisis, but being alone was something I needed to get used to.

CHAPTER SIX

Layla's worried face hovered over me as I attempted to rest on my hideous plaid couch bed.

"They said the baby's fine. I'm fine. I'm just supposed to rest more." I adjusted the pillow under my lower back and wiggled until it felt right.

"Well, something caused you to get sick. Something caused you all that pain. There has to be some reason behind it."

I knew she felt concerned, but her smothering-mothering style was getting to me. She brushed some wayward hair from my face. My hair had never been very cooperative, always escaping from the clips and rubber bands I used to force it into submission.

"Are you hungry? Thirsty? I can get you whatever you like."

I said a quick prayer for patience. "I'm not hungry and not thirsty. I don't want anything but a nap, Lay. Please. Just let me rest."

"Fine, I'll leave you alone. Forgive me for caring about you." She huffed off to the kitchen area, which was only about four feet away. Ripping a bunch of baby wipes from their container, she set about scrubbing the kitchen counter, miniature appliances, and cabinets.

It was Monday, so the faire was closed. Layla had the entire day – the entire *week* – to play the caregiver to me. I wasn't looking forward to day after day of her undivided attention. Inwardly, I groaned. Curling up on my side and closing my eyes, I tried to think of some way to get her attention focused on something, *anything,* else.

I wished Jack would come by, but he was working extra shifts at the hospital, so he could have weekends off for the Renaissance festival. I knew his absence was to blame for at least part of Layla's agitation, as well as her incessant focus on me.

To be honest, I missed Jack, too. I felt safer having someone with medical knowledge around, just in case something happened again.

It was early afternoon, and though I was tired, the bright sunshine seeping in through the cheap camper blinds made it impossible to fall asleep. Frustrated, I sat up, rubbing my eyes. "I think I'll go for a walk."

"Not by yourself, you aren't."

I sighed. "Seriously, Layla, I'm okay." I wasn't sure I could handle seven more months of Layla's hovering, especially when a large portion of it would take place in these cramped quarters. I slipped on my flip flops and stepped outside.

It looked like such a beautiful day. The sun, so irritating when I was trying to sleep, filled me with warmth and strength. I stretched my arms above my head and felt the kinks in my back dissolve. Turning, I headed toward the forest, hoping I would bump into Gibble. Behind me, I heard the camper door slam. Within seconds, another set of footsteps had joined my own.

We walked quietly together for several moments, following the twisting, turning dirt paths in the woods. Everything seemed so different when the festival wasn't open. Calmer. The air tasted purer. Even the trees seemed more relaxed. Various artisans were at their shops, working on building up more inventory. Most waved at us or smiled as we passed them. Though like us, they wore their everyday clothes instead of costumes, or *garb*, as they called it, there was still an ethereal feel to the forest and its goings-on.

We stopped to say hello to Grok and Bork, the two tall, startlingly handsome men who played the roles of the forest gnomes. Grok had a dimple in his right cheek, and sparkling green eyes. They resembled each other a bit. Must be brothers, I thought. I never saw one without the other. Bork was the quieter of the two.

Grok was extremely attractive. Simply the act of shaking his hand left me feeling wobbly-kneed, and I wondered several things in rapid succession. *How bad does my hair look? Is he single? Does he like kids?* It was the third question in my mind that stopped me from making googly eyes at the guy. This wasn't the time to start a new relationship. I could barely handle my life as it was.

Still, though. He was awfully cute.

As we prepared to walk away, Grok pulled me into a hug, squeezing me tight. "Glad to meet you, Keisha," he said. "Welcome to our little Rennie family."

I could feel the heat rising to my cheeks. "Same to you. I mean, I'm glad to meet you, too. I guess I don't need to welcome you to the family. Since you're already here." Oh, my *God*. I wished someone would stick a tree branch into my mouth and make me stop talking.

Finally, we were down the path, turning in a different direction. If I had hoped Layla hadn't noticed my idiocy back there with the Hot Gnome Brothers, I was sadly mistaken.

She punched me in the arm. Not hard, just in her usual, playful fashion. "So, Grok's hot, right?" she asked, eyes sparkling with laughter.

"Maybe a little," I mumbled, embarrassed. This pregnancy thing was making my emotions jump all over the place. Two weeks ago, I was crying into my pillow at night, missing my alcoholic, abusive ex- boyfriend. Now I was making an idiot of myself in front of the first guy I found attractive.

"Bad news for you, hon. Grok's taken."

"Oh." I considered that for a moment. "Well, it's not like I would have… " *Actually slept with him right out the gate. Or have any business getting into a relationship right now.*

"I know."

"It's just that I…" *Am so lonely. I miss having a boyfriend. Even though Vince was a complete ass, I still miss him.*

"Keisha. I know." She slung her arm around my shoulders, and we continued to walk.

That was the thing about Layla. She really did know me. She understood.

I felt surprised at how much of the festival grounds I hadn't seen while I'd been working at the shop. The forest was much larger than I had thought, and there were multiple stores I hadn't noticed over the weekend. "It's so pretty here," I said out loud, though I was really talking to myself. We had just passed a horde of butterflies. It was a common enough sight, and I wondered what in the forest drew so many butterflies to it. I'd never seen such a congregation of tiny airborne rainbows in one place before.

"I know it is," Layla replied. "I love coming up here. I miss the woods when I'm back at home."

A shaft of sunlight was shining in through the trees, landing on a spot just a few feet ahead of us. Tiny shimmers filled the beam, and I walked toward it, my hand outstretched. The simple beauty of it, the warmth, drew me to it, and I ached to stand inside the light. I took one step, then another.

I was falling.

Literally falling. Into a hole.

I landed face first in a pile of twigs and branches. Turned out, it wasn't such a deep hole, only about three feet into the ground. Covered in sticks and mud.

"Keisha! Oh, my God, are you okay?" Layla was pulling at my arms, twisting my head to check my face, dragging me upward.

The teensy smidgeon of dignity I'd had left was bruised for certain. "I give up on life, I think," I said, wiping a dried leaf from my mouth. "Just leave me here in the hole."

"Come on, let me help you up." Layla grabbed me by the wrists and yanked me to my feet.

I stood, half-heartedly brushing dirt and sticks from my clothes, staring blankly at the mess I'd fallen into. "Is there a reason for this death trap?" It seemed like a lawsuit waiting to happen, especially given the amount of little kids running around during the festival.

"Actually, there is. It's the Troll Hole. Gibble does a whole skit with it, two o'clock every day we're open. It's pretty funny, really, if you ever stop to watch it."

"After my brush with death in it, I doubt I'll find it amusing. Management should put some kind of flares around it, before the wrong person falls in and they end up getting sued."

We resumed our walk. A light breeze ruffled the leaves, and I was grudgingly once again aware of the stunning beauty of the forest.

"Honestly, Keisha, you're the first person I've ever heard of falling into it. Maybe you should try being a little more careful. Especially given your current delicate condition." She raised her brows and looked down her nose at me.

"It's like you're *trying* to get me to punch you, Lay. Do you *want* to get punched?" I balled a fist and made a slow-motion punch in her direction.

Layla laughed and put her hands up in mock surrender. "Yeah. I'm so scared. Please don't hit me, scary lady."

My determination not to laugh failed me, and the two of us dissolved into a fit of giggles.

Out of nowhere, an uneasy feeling washed over me and I stopped, looking around for the source of my discomfort. A slight cramping sensation shot through my abdomen and disappeared as fast as it had come on.

Picking up her pace, Layla cupped her hand around my arm and hurried me along.

"Why are we hurrying?" I asked. We had no place to rush off to, as far as I knew.

"Just walk. Don't look at her." Layla's face was determined, her eyes narrowed to slits.

"At who?" Allowing myself to be dragged along, I gazed around anyway. Didn't see much of anything other than the small shack with the sign, "Wicked Witch of the Faire" outside it. The sign was shiny black with fancy cursive letters, and the post it was on seemed to be shaped like an upside-down broomstick, shoved into the ground.

"The witch. Cordelia."

The witch? I hadn't yet met her, but had seen her walking through the faire over the previous weekend. An older woman with long white hair streaked with bright blue, she gave off a strange vibe, for sure, but then lots of people at the festival were a little weird.

We were well past the shack, but still, Layla clung to my arm, her long nails digging into my skin.

"You got some kind of issue going on with her? And let go of my arm. You're hurting me." I pulled, and she released me. I rubbed at the marks left on my flesh from her fingernails. "Ouch."

"Sorry." Layla didn't look sorry. She looked… frightened?

"What's your deal with the witch lady?" Layla was not the sort of person to scare easily. The two of them must've really gotten into it over something.

Layla shrugged. "She's just, um, not very nice. Stay away from her. Promise me you won't go near her."

This was beyond strange. What was one old lady with blue hair going to do to me? But Layla's face seemed so earnest, so legitimately frightened, that I found myself nodding slowly. "Okay, Lay. Okay. I won't." Something scurried across my foot, and I yelped, jumping back. "Oh my God, what was that?" I looked toward a cluster of trees where the whatever-it-was had run off to. "Was it a rat? Oh, my God. Please don't say it was a rat." I bent down, swiping at my foot, like I could get the rodent germs off it that way.

A funny little smile spread across Layla's face. "I think we've spent enough time in the forest today. Don't want to wear you out, Keisha. Tell you what, let's go back to the camper and I'll fix you some lunch."

I *was* feeling a little tired out, especially after that bad cramping feeling I'd experienced just a few minutes before.

Probably shouldn't overdo. "I think you're right. Maybe I'll read a book while you slave away for me in the castle kitchen."

"Keisha? You've got a visitor." Layla winked at me.

I stood up from the couch, brushing imaginary wrinkles from my clothes. I expected Dread Pirate Jack had stopped by to check in on me after his shift at the hospital, and as the camper door swung out, I searched the area around us for his familiar frame. Dusk had fallen, and the pinks and oranges of the evening sky were giving way to pure darkness. The absence of streetlights or buildings in the camping area meant the black of night was complete.

The only person I saw was some tiny guy in jeans and a plaid western-style shirt. His back was to me, so I said, "Hello? Were you looking for me?" I squinted into the last dwindling bit of light.

The man turned around, grinning widely, and seemed familiar, somehow. "Keisha!" His voice sounded deep and thick.

Then as he walked toward me, the feeling of familiarity grew stronger. I must have met him during the festival, because I didn't know anyone else in the area. Layla must have known who he was or she would have sent him packing.

"I wanted to stop and check in on you, see how you were doing after your scare last weekend."

He'd come closer, and I hopped down the camper steps to the ground. So he'd been around when I'd gotten sick and gone off in the ambulance. I sifted through the names of people I'd met at the festival, trying to make one fit this short and oddly attractive man before me.

He was bald. At least, nearly so. A bit of fuzzy stubble lined his head. His smile was wide and genuine, though his teeth were all kinds of crooked. He stuck his hand out and I took it and shook, all the while still looking hard at his face.

It *was* familiar. I'd spoken with this man before, I felt certain of it.

His eyes were the most beautiful color of green, the lashes long and almost girlish.

The name popped out of my mouth before I had time to stop and think, "Gibble?"

It couldn't be. Could it? The funny little troll with the horrendous underbite?

He laughed. "Didn't recognize me, eh? I know I look a little different when I'm out of character."

Still working to reconcile the two sides of this man in my mind, I opened and shut my mouth a couple of times. Finally, I shook some sense into my head and greeted him properly. "Thanks for stopping by, Gibble. How thoughtful of you." I indicated the two fold-up chairs Layla and I kept set up outside the camper.

We both sat. The sun dropped further into the night, and our conversation was lit mainly by the interior of the camper.

I waved at my head. "Your hair is so different!" For starters. And the nasty yellow teeth.

I was remarkably relieved those weren't real.

He chuckled. "Oh, yeah." Rubbing the top of his nearly-bare head, he commented, "That's a wig. Much less there in reality."

Turned out, Gibble had a nice-shaped head. The loss of hair didn't look so bad on him. And when we were sitting down, the difference in our heights didn't seem quite so noticeable.

It was Thursday, and I hadn't seen him since the whole ambulance debacle the weekend before. "Where have you been all week? Do you live far from here?" Some of the vendors and cast lived near the festival, and just went home through the week. Some of them lived and worked hours away, and made the long drive home each Sunday night, only to return at the end of the week.

"Oh, not so far way, I guess. Half hour or so. But I can't cancel classes, so I go ahead and make the drive each week."

"Classes? What do you teach? Aren't you almost out for the summer?" Questions fired out of me like balls from a cannon. I hadn't realized how starved I was for a conversation that wasn't with Layla, and didn't revolve around my alcoholic ex-boyfriend or how to make fairy wings.

"I teach year-round, so no, no summer break for me. Martial arts. I work with under-privileged kids in the city. It's good for them." He paused and made a noise that was half-laugh, half-cough. "It's good for me, as well."

I felt startled at this revelation. If I'd had to lay money on it, I would have bet he taught history. Or maybe math. Gibble seemed more than a little on the dorky side. But martial arts? "That's interesting." I knew nothing at all about martial arts of any sort, so I had nothing else to offer. To be honest, I didn't really think it all that interesting.

"Are you doing okay, then, Keisha? You gave us all a scare when you got sick so suddenly. I hadn't realized you were ill when you were sick back in the trees. Thought it was just the heat, or I would have gone for Jack right away."

His tone was so apologetic, I felt guilty for not telling him about the baby. But not guilty enough not to lie. Layla and Jack had promised not to tell, at least not just yet, and I wasn't ready to explain my screw up of a life to anyone else. "They couldn't say what was wrong for sure. Maybe a combination of the heat and exhaustion. A couple bags of IV fluids and rest got me feeling better." Actually, what the doctor had said was that I could be threatening to miscarry, and needed to rest more and reduce the stress in my life. Yeah, sure. Easy enough for the doctor to say. "Maybe I should lay off the chili bowls," I joked.

Gibble didn't laugh. Instead, he leaned in closer toward me, his big green eyes filled with concern. He took my hand in his, and squeezed. "Please get your rest," he said fervently. "You can't care for anyone else if you don't care for yourself first."

What a strange thing for him to say. And what did he mean, I couldn't care for anyone else? I wasn't showing yet. He couldn't possibly know I was pregnant. But he seemed so earnest, so caring, that I found myself staring straight into his beautiful green eyes. "I will," I replied. "I promise. Besides, Layla is taking good care of me."

"I'm sure," he said agreeably. "She's a good girl."

We sat in silence for a few minutes, until Layla clanged the metal door open, climbed down to sit on the steps, and with her usual loud candor, dove into our quiet conversation, her laughter seeming to fill the darkness around us.

It was a good feeling, having friends.

The longer I was away from Vince, the safer and more content I felt.

CHAPTER SEVEN

"I can go by myself, Layla. I'm grown." I held out my hand and expected her to give me back my purse and keys.

"You are *not* going by yourself. What if you get sick again, and need medical help?" She clutched my bag in her hand, squeezing until her fingers blanched. Thrusting her chin up at me, daring me to yank my purse back, she narrowed her eyes and waited.

I sighed. She was stubborn as all get out…one of the problems I had with Layla.

She wasn't going to go for it. And I needed her van, because my car was still back at her house. My first prenatal appointment was in a few hours, and I didn't want to be late. For all I knew, the doctor could fire me or something for not showing up on time. "Fine." So aggravating. "And you're sure you can't come with me?" Sure, I'd gotten to know some of the faire people over the last couple of weeks, but I wasn't so close to any of them that I wanted them to come to this sort of private appointment with me.

Jack was an option, maybe. At least, he already knew about the baby, and was a trusted medical professional. "Is Jack working at the hospital today?" She would have to know his work schedule. I thought they must have forgotten the idea of going slow with their relationship, because they texted constantly and more than once, I had wakened in the middle of the night to find Layla had disappeared from the camper. I was positive if I looked out the little window over the combination table-bed, I would see Pirate Jack's trailer rocking. And I would not, for any reason, go a'knocking.

"I'm sorry, he does have to work this morning. And I can't go because there is a vendor meeting at the pub, and it's mandatory."

I knew she wanted to come. She was so excited about the baby. Some days, I think she felt more excited than I did.

Not that I wasn't looking forward to having the baby. I just kept a tight, cold guard around my raw heart. It would be too hard for me to let that kind of feeling in, when I kept thinking something might go wrong.

I threw my hands up, exasperated. "Well, then, who else can go?" Because I certainly wasn't taking Cordelia the creepy blue-haired witch with me. My stomach cramped up every time I got near her. The woman gave me the heebie-jeebies.

Layla took a deep breath. "Now, don't get mad, okay?"

"What did you do, Lay?"

"Gibble can go with you." Taking a step back, she looked like she thought I might attack her.

"Gibble." He seemed like a genuinely nice guy, and I didn't hate the idea, but the thought of Layla going behind my back to set it up pissed me off. "So, you've already had this conversation with him. Before you had it with me." I could feel the muscles in my upper back knotting up.

"I'm sorry, Keisha. I thought it would be easier for you if I had it all taken care of." She peeked out the window above her table-bed and smiled. Handing me back the keys and my purse, she continued, "He's here, ready to go."

"Layla." She felt concerned, I got that, but taking liberties to orchestrate my life was taking the smothering-mothering thing a little bit too far. And she didn't look a bit sorry. She looked like the canary-eating cat. "You can't just keep doing these things. You don't get to run my life."

"I'm not trying to *run* it. I'm trying to *fix* it." She smiled brightly at me. "He's waiting, and you'll be late for your appointment if you don't leave now."

Outside the camper, I could hear Gibble whistling a bouncy tune. Squeezing my eyes shut tight, I took a few long, deep breaths. In my nose, out my mouth. I pursed my lips and blew out hard. I gripped the keys in my hand. "Do not," I stated, my jaw tight, "do this again."

"I hear you, I hear you." She held up her hands in mock surrender.

I let the metal door slam behind me as I walked out.

Gibble whistled. A lot.

In fact, I had turned off the van radio because he kept whistling tunes contrary to what was playing. If the song on the radio was fast, he whistled something slow and mournful. When the station played something slow and serious, his tunes became bouncy and fast.

It was annoying, but he had given up his day to ride to my doctor appointment with me, and I didn't want to complain. I just shut off the radio. And occasionally ground my teeth.

The further we drove downstate, the darker the skies became. Heavy clouds fat with moisture loomed lower and lower.

At least, the morning sickness had seemed to abate the last couple of days. That was one positive thing to hang on to. I wondered absently where I could stop for a bowl of chili on the way back.

I cleared my throat.

His whistling paused.

"I was going to tell you. You know, about the baby." I kept my eyes trained on the miles of expressway ahead of me. The trees along the sides of the road created the feeling of being in a tunnel.

Metaphor for my life. One way. One track.

No way out.

I shook my head slightly.

Gibble drummed his fingers on his knee. "Are you trying to apologize for something?"

Shrugging, I checked my rearview mirror and moved to the next lane. "I just mean, I was going to tell you, but Layla beat me to it. I haven't told many people yet. I'm kind of going through a tough time."

He nodded. Drummed his fingers. "It's your body. Your baby. Your news. You don't owe me anything, Keisha."

Guilt was one of my easiest emotions. Guilt for the way my mother ended up. Guilt for the way things went with Vince. Guilt for being pregnant and being stuck in a situation I increasingly felt I had no control over.

I had been alone, or mostly alone, so much in my life. Spending time with people – especially large groups of people – made me feel extremely uncomfortable. And awkward. Layla was easier to be around, because she was loud and vivacious and dragged me out of my shell. Now out of my relationship with Vince for several weeks, I was beginning to see how much he'd taken advantage of my introverted nature. Looking back, it became clear to me, my entire life revolved around him and his drinking, with occasional visits with Layla or my grandmother, Mim.

He had held me back a lot in life. I wished I'd seen it sooner.

But if I had, I wouldn't be on my way to a prenatal appointment. And if Vince had given me nothing else over the last five years, at least I had this. "To be honest, I'm not all that great with people. I'm not like Layla."

Gibble remained silent.

The clouds let loose and rain pummeled the windshield. Flicking on the wipers, I squinted, focusing on staying in my lane, and on the mess of emotions currently bursting out of my mouth, "But I would like to think we are becoming friends, you and I." I squeezed the steering wheel until my fingers began to blanch. "And friends tell each other important things. Right? So I would have told you this. Layla just jumped right in, though."

"I think you're—"

In The Presence Of Knowing

Gibble leaned toward me, and I felt like he was trying to have a moment with me, but now that the floodgates had been unlocked, I just kept blabbering, "And you're a great guy, a nice guy, I knew that from the beginning. I *want* you and I to become good friends. Great friends! I need more friends. I tend to keep myself isolated, but I'm not sure that's always the healthiest thing. Especially…"

Now he seemed nervous. Jumpy. His hands fluttered before landing firmly against his knees. "Keisha, I think you're—"

I was going to say something to him I hadn't shared yet with anyone, but I felt sharing something really personal with Gibble would help solidify our burgeoning friendship. I remembered the day I was so sick, puking in the forest, alone. Gibble had been there. He had barely known me, but he had shown up and held me through my struggle.

More than my own mother had ever done.

I gulped, intent on saying the thing that had been tormenting my mind for weeks. "Just let me finish, please. I need another friend, especially since I think there might be something wrong with the baby." Blowing out a breath, I waited for his response. I hadn't said anything to Layla yet about the dreams, or the frightening feeling of foreboding that often came on the heels on my thoughts about the tiny human growing inside me.

I wasn't sure exactly how I had expected him to respond. To be honest, I had hoped for him to slide his hand across the van console and take mine in his. Or a pat on the shoulder, maybe, some sort of small physical connection to let me know I wasn't as alone in this situation as I felt I was.

But of the myriad of possibilities, I am certain I didn't expect him to scream.

"KEISHA!" he hollered, straining against his seatbelt.

I jumped, positive some car was sliding through the rain, about to hit us. Looking around frantically for the threat, gooseflesh rippling down my arms, I saw nothing that would warrant his reaction. "What? What is it?" My heart was hammering and I was not entirely certain I hadn't peed myself a little bit.

In my defense, it had been a long, long drive and we hadn't stopped for any bathroom breaks.

"You missed the exit," he mumbled, sitting back against his seat and rubbing his forehead. He pulled out his phone and, I assumed, activated his GPS. "Get off at the next exit. We can still make it on time if we don't have any more distractions."

I felt beyond stupid. I'd been so involved with pouring out my heart, I'd nearly gotten us lost.

That, right there, is exactly why it was better for everyone if I just stayed away from people.

My presence only screwed things up.

In this area of Illinois, there were few physicians who accepted state insurance. My options limited, I'd gone with the one who had the least awful online reviews.

The office seemed to emit a slight smell of mildew. Not terrible, but it made me think there had at some point been a leak and it hadn't been cared for properly. The waiting room chairs were upholstered in that particular shade of green popular in the 1970's.

We weren't in the waiting room long, however. My slip-up on the expressway had left us pulling in to the doctor's office parking lot with three whole minutes to spare until my appointment time. Other than reading me directions from his phone, Gibble hadn't said much to me since my little—whatever it was.

Outburst. Confession.

Maybe we hadn't been getting as close as I'd hoped we were.

Still, when the nurse called my name, I stood and reached behind me for Gibble's hand.

In The Presence Of Knowing

I'd been mad when I found out Layla had gone behind my back, orchestrating Gibble's presence at my appointment today. But now, faced with the possibility this unfamiliar doctor could do some test and tell me today that something was definitely wrong with my baby, I felt beyond grateful to have him with me.

Gibble laced his hand through mine, walking beside me, and the warmth of his hand in mine made me feel stronger. More capable.

Whatever the doctor had to say, I could do this. Even if, as I suspected, something was terribly wrong.

The office clearly wasn't new or even recently refurnished, but the air conditioning unit was working overtime. I sat on the exam table, shivering in my thin paper gown.

"Do you want me to stay?" With his back ramrod straight, his eyes narrowed, and his jaw obviously tight, he looked like a man on an unpleasant mission, but willing to soldier through.

For the sake of his country. Or the weird pregnant fairy chick he'd recently gotten stuck with babysitting.

The thing was, I could see he felt uncomfortable, but I didn't want him to leave. Call me selfish.

It's not the worst thing I've ever been called.

"I wish you would," I said softly, my voice barely more than a whisper. "I'm a little bit scared."

For the most part, I'd grown up alone. My mother had her own problems, and I was just a gnat circling the air, I think, for most of my childhood. She couldn't quite swat me away, but she hadn't embraced me, either. Mim tried, but she was old and often confused.

Vince had done very little to try to support me in my hardest moments, despite the way I clung to him during his various struggles. Layla, of course, had always been there, as much as she could be. But, much like the emotional and occasional physical abuse from Vince I didn't talk about, Layla couldn't help me with the pain I kept to myself.

I could deal with a lot of hard things on my own. I'd become used to it. But just this once, I needed someone to see my vulnerability, to be the strong one for me. I wanted someone who could hold me up if I needed to lean on them.

Even if that someone was eight inches shorter and probably fifty pounds lighter than me.

I knew it had to be embarrassing for Gibble as the doctor rummaged around down under my gown, but he stood tall – well, as tall as he could – and held my hand for the duration, occasionally using his other hand to pat my shoulder.

Now and again, his cheeks flamed red.

I felt more uncomfortable than embarrassed. Because I needed to pee, and the doctor's hand was pressing against places that made me need to pee even more. I'd also become more tense, waiting for him to find out something terrible had gone wrong.

Dr. Griffith was an aging, white-haired man with wireframe glasses which sat low on his nose.

I stared at Gibble's face as Dr. Griffith stood and peeled off his latex gloves. Having my legs spread open in the presence of the doctor and Gibble hadn't bothered me so much.

Somehow, watching the man cheerily discard the gloves he'd used to probe around inside me, bothered me a whole lot more.

Gibble met my gaze and held steady, his hand still strong, squeezing mine.

"You can sit up now, Miss Keisha." The doctor's voice sounded rumbly, the way I imagined Santa Clause's voice would be.

Sliding a hand beneath my back without being asked to do so, Gibble helped push me up to a sitting position. I fiddled awkwardly with the hem of my paper dress.

Scribbling on my chart, Dr. Griffith peppered me with questions, "Morning sickness trouble you much?" He peered at me over the rim of his glasses.

"Some," I replied. I couldn't explain why I said that if I had to, because I'd been sick an awful lot. But I felt this inherent sense of guilt that told me Dr. Griffith would be burdened by my sickness if I was honest about it. So I lied.

I felt more than saw Gibble's head swivel in my direction. His hand grasped mine once again, and he squeezed my fingers. *Hard.* He cleared his throat.

"Okay, a little more than some, I guess. I throw up a lot. It's been a bit better the last few days, though."

Nodding, the doctor asked, "Some? A lot? Define that, please. How many times in a day?" He paused writing, his pen hovering above my chart.

"Oh. Once or twice, maybe." I blinked hard, as my fingers were in the process of getting crushed again. I coughed. "Once or twice, in the morning." I glared at the man by my side who was supposed to be supporting me, instead of breaking my fingers and forcing me into honesty with the doctor. "And sometimes, a few times at night."

I was startled when Gibble spoke up, "She's lost weight. I think she's been sick more than what's normal. Two weeks ago, she collapsed in the middle of the day and had to be taken by ambulance to the hospital."

Now, I was the one squeezing his fingers. My hands were bigger than his.

I hoped fervently that I could break at least one of them.

"I see," Dr. Griffith replied. "And what did the doctor at the hospital say?"

"He said I was fine," I blurted, and turned my attention to the traitor beside me. "How would you even know if I've lost weight?" I hissed at him.

"Because I pay attention!" he whispered back. He focused on the physician. "The ER doctor said she was dehydrated, needed more rest, and could be threatening to miscarry."

Still whispering angrily at the traitor, I asked, "How do you even know all that? I didn't tell anyone!"

The jerk troll smirked at me. "I talked to Jack."

Dr. Griffith cut in, "Wait. Who is Jack?"

"The pirate," we both said at once.

"Well, that clears things up, doesn't it?" the doctor said, his voice loud and jolly. His demeanor said he'd seen and heard it all in his many years of practice, and one awkward, vertically mismatched couple with an apparent pirate fetish didn't startle him all that much. "Keisha, I can tell you that I see nothing on exam today that concerns me. You and your baby seem just fine, although I will prescribe you some Zofran to help with the nausea and vomiting. You're just about at the end of your first trimester, so the morning sickness should settle down before too much longer."

I hadn't realized how tight the muscles in my back had gotten until he said this. "Really? That's wonderful!" I would be able to eat as much chili as I wanted. And it would stay put! Briefly, I fantasized about consuming a vat of super spicy chili with shredded cheese on top. My mouth watered at the thought of it.

"We've lost your wife to sweeter thoughts, I'm afraid."

Dr. Griffith's voice cut through the chili-fog in my brain. My eyes shot to Gibble's face, which was apparently fighting not to dissolve into laughter.

His green eyes bright and merry, he looked on the verge of exploding with hysteria.

I realized I had been licking my lips.

And wait. Had he just referred to me as Gibble's *wife*?

The doctor had a contraption of some sort in his hands. He grinned at me. "If you'll lie back, we will listen to the heartbeat."

I obeyed, listening intently through the whooshing sound for something that resembled a beating heart.

It wasn't there.

The same way I had shut my emotions off when Vince had attacked me, I flicked an imaginary switch in my mind, shielding my heart from whatever bad news was coming. Gibble had taken my hand again, but I didn't squeeze it this time. My fingers sat in his hand, limp and still. I took a long, deep breath.

Beside me, the doctor sighed heavily as he pressed his device against different places on my abdomen.

He furrowed his brows and tilted his head, trying again and again.

Watching his face was making me think all sorts of terrible thoughts. I turned my head to Gibble.

His green eyes fixed on my brown ones. He didn't blink. Just stood there, strong and steady. "It's okay, it's okay," he whispered, never breaking my gaze.

"There it is!" Dr. Griffith looked visibly relieved. "Listen."

Sure enough, through the repetitive whooshing sound was another noise. *Thump-thump, thump-thump.*

Bit by bit, the icy shield I'd thrown over my heart began to melt.

"Sounds perfect. I'd like you to come back in a month, Keisha." He cleaned off the device and set it aside, picking up my chart again to document my information. "Call if anything seems out of the ordinary. Bleeding, intense cramping, or if the medicine I'm giving you doesn't help with the nausea and vomiting."

"All right." I felt stunned that the doctor didn't think anything was wrong. Squeezing my eyes shut, I replayed the doctor's words over and over in my mind. *Sounds perfect.* Could I believe that? The sense of foreboding was so strong, so real. Maybe it was just me expecting pain and loss. It's been so ingrained in me, I was having a hard time believing something good was happening.

The doctor left, and something wet splashed onto my hand.

Gibble's big green eyes were overflowing. Tears dripped down his cheeks, running off his chin and falling onto my hand.

I returned his earlier words to me, "It's okay, it's okay."

He dragged the backs of his hands across his eyes, nodding his head as he sniffed. He managed a watery smile. "I've got a tendency toward the emotional, you see," he said, trying to laugh it off. "Always have tended to be overly sensitive. Apologies."

But it pricked something deep inside me, and I could feel warmth seeping through the final remnants of my icy heart.

It seemed like the most normal thing in the world when I sat up on the exam table and drew him toward me, paper dress and all. With his head against my chest, I brushed my palm across the stubble on the crown of his head. To think how he'd become so emotional over my baby and me – me, who had been so easy for my mother to abandon, who'd been so easy for Vince to use as a punching bag – made me feel like maybe happiness was something feasible I could reach for.

Maybe even attain.

His tears continued to flow onto my gown, the thin, crinkly paper of it sticking to the skin of my chest.

"Gibble?" I said, my voice low. The staff would be expecting me to exit the room shortly.

He sniffed, and stood back, turning his head away from me.

"I need to get dressed. Could you…?" I slid off the exam table, bending down to grab my leggings and oversized shirt. Pressing my clothes against my chest to hide the fact that the paper gown was drenched and see-through, and I wore nothing beneath it, I stood against the table while he passed me to get to the door. As he walked by me, I became painfully aware of the fact that my breasts had grown larger over the last couple of weeks.

Gibble stopped, holding his hand out in my direction. His red-rimmed eyes flitted away from mine. "If you give me your keys, I'll pull the van around, so you don't have to walk as far."

Now, I was the one who wanted to cry.

But I didn't. I held my emotions in check and handed over the keys.

CHAPTER EIGHT

"Do you need to get right back, or do you have enough time for me to make a stop?" I took a swig from the water bottle in the van console as we waited at a red light.

One shoulder raised up, then dropped. "Nothing so exciting it can't wait for a bit. I do have a class to teach tonight, but not until eight. There's time if you need to stop."

At least the rain had let up, though the skies were still gray. With Dr. Griffith's assurance about the baby doing all right, I felt lighter. Happier. And I wanted to share my news with Mim. "It won't take long. I just want to stop and tell my grandmother about the baby." I turned left off the street that would have taken us back to the expressway. "I hadn't had a chance to let her know yet."

"Is it that you hadn't had the chance, or that you didn't want to tell anyone about the baby when you thought something was wrong?"

Funny thing about Gibble. It's like he could see into my mind when I hadn't even fully articulated a thought yet. Here he was again, pushing me to be honest with myself.

"Probably some of both. She's old and has lost so much already. I didn't want to give her something else she loved, only to lose it." Turning down Mim's little side street, I eased my foot off the gas pedal. "Be there in a minute."

"You haven't talked much about your family. Are you parents... gone?"

I pulled into Mim's drive and put the van in park. I wanted to be irritated, but the expression on his face told me he wasn't being nosy. He just cared, and maybe this was something I needed to get used to. Shifting a bit in my seat, so I could look directly at him, I replied, "Are we doing a family genealogy pop quiz now?" I said, deliberately keeping my voice light. "My dad wasn't interested in sticking around. My mother is a homeless drug addict. I rarely see her. Mim is who mostly raised me, and just about all the family I have. Besides the obvious, of course." I patted my belly and threw the question back at him. "How about you? What about your family?"

His eyes shuttered for a brief second, then opened wide. He sprawled his palms on his knees and pressed down. "Easy answer. They're all gone."

Empathy filled my chest, making it ache. I hadn't expected that and felt guilty for asking so flippantly. "I'm so sorry, Gibble. I didn't realize."

Gibble rubbed his face and stared out the window. "It's all right. It's been a long time ago, now."

We trudged up the driveway in silence. As I rang the doorbell, I heard him say quietly, "I guess we are much the same that way. Alone."

It made me sad, the way he said it, and I wanted to do something to comfort him.

But Mim had opened the door, her rheumy, purple eyes taking in the sight of us. A half-smile on her face, she stepped back and motioned for us to come in. "Kelly?" her voice trembled as she called me by my mother's name. She shook her head, which was covered in a cloud of snow white curls. "Keisha, I meant to say. And this is?" she asked, looking at Gibble, who stood about a foot behind me.

"Mim, this is my friend…" I realized I didn't know what his actual name was, and I paused.

Gibble stepped forward, taking Mim's hand graciously in his, and covering her hand with his other one. He had excellent posture, I thought, something I, being a lifelong slumper, admired. "Rogan O'Connor," he said with a charming smile. "Such a pleasure to meet you, m'lady."

Mim, who had once been about my height but had shrunk with age, fluttered her eyes at him, clearly smitten. "Rogan? Oh, an Irish boy." She giggled and patted her hair. "I've always liked a nice Irish boy."

Here's the thing about Mim. Back in the day, she'd been a little bit of a party girl. That would also be putting it kindly.

My grandmother had been a slut of epic proportions.

And now she was standing here, hitting on a guy who was totally not my boyfriend, but still.

She was my *grandmother.*

"Mim? Let's sit down, I have something I want to tell you."

Reluctantly disengaging her hand from Gibble's, she tottered off in the direction of the kitchen.

My nice little Irish friend and I took seats on the ancient flowered sofa.

"Rogan, dear, would you like some lemonade?" she called in a voice laced with sugar. We could hear the opening and shutting of cabinets, glasses clanking against the countertop.

"What's her name?" Gibble, or, I guess, Rogan, asked me.

"Katharine. And don't encourage her." Meaningfully raising my eyebrows at him, I gave him a hard look.

"I'd love some lemonade, Katharine, dear!" the traitor called back.

Kicking him wouldn't be out of the realm of propriety, I thought. He'd been going against me all day.

Instead, I replied to the question she hadn't bothered to ask me, "I'd like some as well, Mim!"

With a Cheshire cat grin fixed firmly in place, Rogan accepted the cold glass Mim offered.

She set the tray with my drink and hers down on the coffee table. "Your mother came by this week," she said, and paused, taking a long, slow sip of her lemonade.

I shot a quick glance at Rogan. There was so much still he didn't know about her. "Oh? That's nice. She doing well?" I hoped to high heaven Mim wasn't about to say something to humiliate me.

"Staying with a new friend in Chicago. Considering rehab again."

I read between the lines to hear the things Mim didn't say. Mom was likely whoring herself out for drugs, staying with a pimp. My mother had been "considering rehab" for the last decade at least. Not that she'd ever gone.

"Good for her," I replied politely. I took a quick sip of my drink and set it back down on the tray. Pulling nervously at my long cotton shirt, I summoned a smile. "Mim, I have something to tell you."

Leveling a direct gaze at me with her cloudy, purple eyes, she startled me by saying, "I already know, Keisha."

What? She had to be getting confused again. She couldn't possibly know. "I don't think you do, Mim." I scooted to the edge of the sofa cushion. "First of all, I wanted to let you know that I broke up with Vince. So if he comes around here, tell him to get lost. Or call the cops. Hear me?"

"I hear you, Keisha. It's about time. That one never did treat you right. I won't let him come around here, don't worry."

"And the other thing I need to tell you about is… "I paused for a second, searching for the right words. I didn't want to startle her into having a heart attack or anything.

Mim nodded. "About the baby."

A chill sauntered up my spine. I blew out a deep breath. "How did you know?" I hadn't told anyone but Layla, and it seemed like anyone else I tried to tell already knew. Somehow.

Mim smiled, a creepy expression that spread slowly across her face, as though someone else was pulling up the corners of her mouth. "I just know. And that's the bitch of it, isn't it?" She laughed mirthlessly. "I'll always know. And the curse goes on." Her hand shook as she lifted the glass of lemonade back to her lips, the ice cubes slamming against the sides of the clear cup.

Rogan placed his glass down on the tray next to mine and stood abruptly. "I'm sorry to cut this short, Keisha, but I really do need to get heading back." He turned to Mim. "And truly, so pleased to meet you, Katharine. I hope to have the pleasure again soon."

Rising from my seat, I stepped around the coffee table to wrap Mim in a brief hug. Her statements had unsettled me, and left that dark sense of foreboding in my gut once again. She was getting older and more confused. Likely, my mother's recent visit had gotten her all upset. It wouldn't be much longer, and we would have to talk about selling the old house and getting Mim into some kind of assisted living apartment.

And why did I think the word "we?" There was only me.

Always the one left alone to handle the hard things.

Though the silence in the van as we headed back to Windy Springs seemed companionable, I felt compelled to fill it. After driving for several very quiet minutes, I spoke up, "I'm sorry that was so—weird, Gibble. I mean, Rogan," I corrected. It was going to be difficult to remember to call him by his name, since I now knew it. "The older she gets, the more confused she seems. I worry about her."

"It's fine. I enjoyed meeting your grandmother. I was just a little surprised, I suppose."

"Surprised?" He'd probably imagined her as a fragile little thing tucked in bed. Not a purple-eyed sass-machine who flirted shamelessly with him.

"Ah, well. I guess in my mind, I expected her to look more like you. Good lesson about making assumptions."

Look more like me? Oh, right. *That.*

"You expected her to be black?" I knew he didn't intend to come off as anything other than genuinely curious. Glancing at him from the corner of my eye, I saw him nod. "Nah. My mom is white, and my dad, whoever and wherever he is... is black."

"Does it bother you, for me to say that?"

If he'd acted like a jerk about it, I wouldn't have been so open with him. "I've been fielding questions about my race all my life. It doesn't bother me, as long as the person asking the questions isn't being an ass about it," I replied honestly.

"Hungry?" Rogan must have been uncomfortable, suddenly changing the topic that way. Pointing at a sign up ahead, he said, "Keisha, look. There's a Wendy's off this exit. They've got chili!" Grinning at me, he wiggled his eyebrows.

I laughed. "Chili sounds delightful." I flicked on my blinker, moving onto the exit ramp. At the prospect of food, my stomach rumbled... but thankfully, not in a way that made me want to find a nearby toilet or trashcan.

Rogan offered to pay, and for that, I felt grateful. Even a small expenditure like fast food was tough on my limited budget. He came out with our food, and we remained in the parking lot to eat.

"This isn't quite as good as the kind at Ren faire, but it still tastes good. Thanks for this, Rogan," I said, lifting my bowl in his direction.

"No problem." Taking a bite of his cheeseburger, he stared out the windshield, at the two families with small children coming out of the restaurant.

I wondered about his life. He was older than me, I felt sure of that. Mid-thirties, maybe. Had he always taught martial arts and played a troll at the festival? Had he been married? Had kids? "Tell me about you," I blurted. One way, I guess, to jumpstart a conversation.

He turned to me, his green eyes widened in surprise above the wrapper and last little bite of cheeseburger. He held my gaze as he chewed and swallowed the last of his meal. "About me, huh? Not much to tell. You already know what I do for a living." Slowly, carefully, he crumbled his wrapper and set it inside the paper bag. He whistled a quiet, sad tune.

The need to connect on a deeper level with Rogan was visceral. I felt it, physically felt it, like a sharp pang in my soul. At some point during this drive and my appointment and the bizarre visit with Mim, I'd realized I needed more than just Layla in my life. As much as I loved her, I needed more than her, though my introverted nature typically pulled me back from striking up friendships. I had this innate desire to become closer with Rogan, much closer than just hanging out at Windy Springs or letting him hold my hair when I puked. "Okay, let me tell you something about me, then. I'm twenty-eight, I don't have much of a relationship with my mother, I have one friend, Layla, I recently left my abusive, alcoholic boyfriend and the father of my baby," I paused because saying this out loud still hurt like crazy. "I left my job so he couldn't find me, so now I'm living in a forest pretending to be a fairy.

I tossed my phone in the trash because he wouldn't quit calling and texting me, and I feel so scared and alone that I'm not sure I can handle raising this baby by myself, even though I really, *really,* want to be a good mother." Staring into my nearly empty bowl of chili, I swiped angrily at a lone tear that traveled down my cheek. "And I don't cry, I never cry, because I don't have the choice to ever be weak. I have to be the strong one, and Rogan, I am so tired of being strong and pretending everything is okay." Taking a big gulp of air and rubbing at my eye, I pressed on, the words an avalanche of emotion I couldn't seem to stop. "I'm terrible at making friends, but I want you to be my friend, Rogan. I want to know you, and I want you to know me, and for us to have that relationship, I need to know more about you. Please. Please do this for me, Rogan."

Why did I suddenly have this desire to blab my whole life story to Rogan?

Throughout my entire monologue, he had continued to whistle, but now he stopped, shifting in his seat, so he faced me directly. His fists opened and clenched, and his jaw tightened. "Abusive? This man hurt you?" The green eyes I had thought so pretty earlier in the day when he wept at the good news the doctor gave me, now blazed with fury.

Height notwithstanding, Rogan suddenly possessed the look of a murderous warrior. "Tell me, Keisha."

The look of utter honesty on his face drew me to him. I knew he cared, and I needed to unload. The strain of trying to act happy around Layla and everyone else at Windy Springs was wearing me down.

I told him. It tumbled out in a rush: the years of Vince's failed attempts at sobriety, my failed attempts at saving him, the final few weeks, when he'd struck me and left me bruised and frightened. Then finding out I was pregnant, leaving and showing up at Layla's. Telling my story felt cathartic, and once again, I was thankful I'd gotten stuck on that stupid tree the first day at the festival. If not, I might not have met this man who was becoming an important fixture in my life.

Before I realized what he was doing, Rogan had shoved the remnants of our lunch off the van console that separated us and climbed up on it, wrapping his arms around me and pulling me in to him. He stroked my head, slipping his fingers easily through my hair. He may have been a small man, but his arms were muscular and solid and I felt safe with them wrapped around me. With my head against his chest, I felt him take a deep breath.

"Keisha," he began, his deep voice washing over me in waves of comfort and strength, "I cannot express how sorry I am that you have been through this kind of pain. If I'd known you then, and was aware of what was going on, I would have killed him."

It wasn't what I thought he was going to say, and at first, a laugh bubbled up in my throat at the thought of it. Tiny Rogan pitted against enormous Vince, who was better than six feet tall.

The giggle died out before it ever had the chance to erupt from my mouth, when I remembered the murderous look on Rogan's face just moments before, and considered his martial arts skills. The truth was, I really had no idea what exactly Rogan could do. Maybe he could have killed him.

For a split second, I wished he would have.

"Do you often kill off the enemies of your friends?" I mumbled into the fabric of his shirt.

"Only when absolutely necessary," he replied. He went on, "So, you want to know more about me?"

I nodded, tilting my face upward to look at him. Why this was so very important to me all of a sudden, I couldn't explain. I only knew I needed to know more about him, and I needed this knowledge instantly. Though, I felt in some way that I was demanding a friendship with him whether he wanted it or not, I didn't feel able to stop myself.

"Let's see. How far back do you want me to go?"

I lifted my shoulders and dropped them, shifting slightly, so my head rested against his shoulder. I wanted to see his face more clearly as he talked. I continued to clutch my empty chili bowl in my hands, resting it against my thigh.

"I spent a lot of time in foster care as a kid," he began. "My parents were... not always able to care for me."

He stopped, and though I wanted to comment, I kept my mouth shut.

"It was often difficult, and my physical appearance didn't help matters. Quite frequently, I was a target for those who sought someone weaker and smaller to pick on. At the time, it was a great struggle for me, but eventually it's what brought me to what I do now, teaching kids how to defend themselves."

"I hate that you were bullied. You didn't deserve that." I wished I could go back in time to defend a small, frightened Rogan on the school playground.

Tipping his chin down, he gave me a sad smile. "Does anyone deserve that, really?" After a moment, he picked up his story, "Don't pity me, Keisha. I'm not that frightened child anymore. I grew up... at least, to some extent." He laughed. "I met a girl."

For a second, I thought he was talking about me. But his eyes were seeing something far away, and I knew he visited his past as he spoke. His voice sounded wistful. "Her name was Janna. We were so happy. I thought," he paused, cleared his throat, "I thought she was, as they say, the *one*. But I screwed it up, and she left. It's been five years, and I haven't been with anyone since."

I'd been trying to stay quiet and let him talk, but at that, I sat up and blurted, "Five *years*?"

Rogan released his hold on me and slithered back over to the passenger seat. "Yes, well. It is what it is, I suppose."

Searching for something more appropriate to say, several sentences shot through my mind, from assurances about his appearance to incredibly lame things like, *Don't worry, you'll meet the right one at the right time.*

My intentions must have showed on my face, because Rogan laughed, waving a hand at me. "Let me assure you, I'm not self-conscious about my looks or my height. I made peace with myself a long time ago. Nor is the problem that I can't get a date. I've had plenty of offers. But Keisha..." His voice took on a more serious tone. "I'm not a man who gives myself away lightly. Not in friendship, or in romantic relationships. I would rather wait for what is real, and give it my all."

Flashing back to when I first met him, I remembered thinking of Rogan as "a funny little troll," and as I sat there, listening to this sincere, sensitive, and yes, *attractive* man before me, I could not possibly have been more ashamed of myself. "How did you end up at Windy Springs? Have you worked there long?"

"Oh," he said, fluttering his hand dismissively. "It's fun, and besides, it's good to be around others like me. I've been the troll there for ten years, at least."

I reached over to put my empty chili bowl in Wendy's sack, and turned on the ignition. "Thank you, Rogan, for telling me this. I feel so much closer to you, now. I hope you understand what today has meant to me. I feel less alone. And please know, I don't want this to be a one-sided friendship. I want to be a good, real friend to you as well. I'm—I'm thankful for you." Looking in the rearview mirror as I put the van in reverse, I waited as a black pick-up truck drove slowly behind us.

When the truck finally moved out of our way, I backed out, and turned toward the expressway, content to be on our way to Windy Springs.

In the seat beside me, Rogan whistled. I realized I no longer found his habit irritating in the least.

It wasn't until later that night, as I thought about the things Rogan had said, that I wondered what he meant when he'd said, *"Others like me."*

CHAPTER NINE

Sitting beside Layla in our chairs outside the camper, I happily explained to her what Dr. Griffith had to say at my appointment. Rogan had hung out with us for a while, but had left to make it to his class on time.

"When are you due?" Layla's eyes sparkled the way I had hoped Mim's would when I told her my news.

With my hands on my still-flat belly, I responded, "Mid-November." November thirteenth had been his guess.

"We've got so much to do before then!" Layla bounced in her seat, clapping, her red curls looking like springs in the early evening light. "We'll have to make more space at my house to set up the crib, and plan a baby shower!" She was off and running, her mind obviously full of plans.

"A baby shower?" I laughed. "Seriously, Layla, and invite who? It would be just you and me!"

"Not true! We just need to think it out, and it will be great. Trust me! Besides, we could invite Jack, and Gibble and your mom—"

I stopped her right there, holding up my hand. "We are *not* inviting my mother. Hell, no. And probably not even Mim. I don't think she was very happy about the baby. She said I was just perpetuating a curse, or something." I knew Mim had to have been confused when she said it, but it still stung. She was the only blood family I really had, and I had wanted her to be excited for me.

Scrunching her nose, Layla asked, "Curse? What's that supposed to mean?"

Tossing my hands in the air, I said, "I have no idea. She was agitated. And my mom's been coming around again, which I think gets her upset, you know."

Layla sobered. "I'm sorry, Keisha. I know it upsets you, too."

I sighed. Another happy conversation diverted to sadness and frustration. My mother seemed to have that effect on everything. Picking at the hem of my shirt, I replied, "Yeah. It does. Let's not talk about her any more. New topic! Do we have enough inventory for the shop tomorrow, or do we need to whip up some more wings right quick after dinner?"

To her credit, Layla went along with the new direction of my conversation. "We are all set for tomorrow, I counted them up after the meeting this morning. By next week, you and I are going to have to spend a day or two making more."

"Oh, right. How did your meeting go?" Anything, any topic at all, to keep the discussion from circling back to me and my dysfunctional family.

A shadow passed briefly across her face. Her voice tilted higher. "Oh, it was fine. There's been a little, um, issue, with Cordelia. But the owner, Jack's father, is taking care of it. Or trying to, at least."

Cordelia? The creepy old witch lady? "You know, I don't like that lady. I feel sick to my stomach every time I get near her. She gives off a weird vibe."

Layla had stood and opened the trailer door, but now she paused, one foot on the step. "Remember what I said, Keisha. Stay away from her. I mean it. Promise me?"

I nodded in compliance, but wondered what could possibly be so strange about this woman that Layla would continue to caution me against going near her. What could the old, blue-haired woman do to me? And why would they hold an entire vendor meeting to talk about her? *Weird.* Regardless, the fact was that I had an unpleasant physical reaction whenever I passed by her shack, and would stay away from her based on this fact alone. "Are you making dinner tonight, or are we grabbing some take out?" I called into the camper without moving from my seat. Despite our earlier stop at Wendy's, I was getting hungry again.

"You stay put, Keisha. It won't take me long. I'm making spaghetti!" she called back.

Content, I pulled out the paperback romance novel I'd tucked into my purse.

That was the thing about Layla: She made the best spaghetti ever.

Friday dawned bright and early. After a quick breakfast – between Layla and Rogan, I had a feeling I was never going to be allowed to skip a meal again – I helped Layla get On a Wing and a Prayer set up for business. By this point, we had a routine down and we each set about our tasks quietly.

At least, I was quiet. Forgoing caffeine during pregnancy seemed like a cruel trick. Getting my brain going in the mornings took me a lot longer than usual without my standard glass of Mountain Dew to pep me up. I was also missing my occasional energy drink splurge.

Layla, on the other hand, had already consumed four big cups of coffee. She seemed to be raring to go, her incessant chatter peppering our area of the forest as she worked and talked along with the other vendors and some of the cast who sometimes stopped by.

As I carefully set out the wings for sale, I sipped on a cold green tea with honey and tried to make myself like it. Many caffeine-free mornings stretched out before me like an endless sea. My chest ached at the thought of it.

"Need help?" a deep, familiar voice asked from behind me.

I turned with a smile. "Rogan!" Resisting the urge to throw my arms around him, I instead picked up another set of wings.

In just a few more hours, it would be opening time, and he wasn't yet in his troll costume. In a pair of cargo shorts and t-shirt, he looked so normal it was hard to believe in just a few hours he would be transformed into a filthy troll with a bad underbite.

I hadn't costumed up yet, either, and was dressed just in jean shorts and a tank top. It wouldn't be much longer, I thought, and I would need to start buying bigger clothes. "Could you carry that box of wings over here for me?" I pointed to our wagon, filled with boxes of merchandise. "You're here early."

"Yeah. I wanted to talk to the owner about the meeting yesterday, find out what all was going on." Rogan carried the box of wings toward me, setting them down in the dirt next to my flip-flop-clad feet.

"Oh… I thought that was just for the vendors?" I hated to think I'd made him miss something important. Guilt had become my standard emotion, and I'd become used to it creeping up on me this way, pervading most of my thoughts.

"It was. I'm just nosy." He flashed me a grin. "Eat yet?"

At this offer, I now truly felt like I was wearing a sign that read, "Feed me."

Pushing some wayward black tendrils back from my face, and hanging up another set of wings on a peg on the outside of the hut, I replied, "I had some cereal before I left the camper. Boss lady won't let me come to work if I don't eat something first." I rolled my eyes and tipped my head in Layla's direction.

"Smart boss lady." He picked up a set of wings from the box and spun in a slow circle. "If I help you finish setting up, would you like to grab a bite to eat before opening?"

I considered the absence of a tummy-tsunami this morning. Five lucky, food-filled days in a row. I had the feeling I'd better take advantage of the ability to keep food down while it lasted. "Sure thing. Here, if you can get this box of stuff set out on that table over there, I think we can leave the rest for Layla." I pointed in her direction.

She had totally ceased helping me and instead, seemed to be engaged in a deep conversation with the Dread Pirate Jack and the gnomes, Grok and Bork. They huddled in a little group several feet away from On a Wing and a Prayer, talking intensely.

As we finished setting up the shop, Layla wandered back toward us, as her entourage scattered into different areas of the forest. She seemed distracted by something, and her eyebrows were furrowed, creating tiny lines across the bridge of her nose.

I put out the last set of wings from the boxes I was emptying, and caught her attention. "Hey, Lay? Rogan is taking me to get a bite."

Her eyes shuttered for a split second before she spoke, "Rogan? Who is that?"

At first, I thought she was joking, but she wasn't. She really didn't know.

"Rogan? You know… Gibble? The troll?" Seriously? Layla had been working with the guy for how many years and she didn't know his real name? I jerked my thumb in his direction.

Recognition flashed across her face. "Oh, right. Gibble." She waved a dismissive hand toward me. "You two have fun. Don't forget we open at eleven, so be back before then. I'll finish up here." Bending down, she opened another cardboard box, carefully extracting an ornate set of bronze wings.

It bothered me how Layla seemed so dismissive of Rogan. Sure, she thought he was a nice guy, but as far as she was concerned, he was mainly just part of the colorful backdrop at Windy Springs Renaissance Festival.

She couldn't see what I did; a kind, generous, attractive man.

A man, I found, had been dominating my thoughts with increasing frequency.

A man who was so much more than just the funny little troll at the Ren faire.

The Soup and a Song place hadn't gotten their gigantic vat of chili cooked yet, and my stomach was filled with sadness.

Of course, it was only nine in the morning, but still, a chili bread bowl had been the thing I yearned for.

Bereft of my first and favorite choice, I stood in the center of the food court, undecided.

"Options are a good thing. Try mixing it up a little bit, so you don't get bored of it." Rogan already knew what he wanted, I could tell, but he was politely – if not patiently – waiting for me to make up my mind. He tapped his foot against the ground as he stood staring at a place called What Came First? which, as its name implied to the observant viewer, sold both chicken and eggs, all day long in a variety of forms.

I let him stew just a few minutes longer, watching with immense amusement as he rubbed his nearly-bald head in agitation. Taking pity on my new friend, I said, "You know, you're right. Maybe eggs are the way to go this morning." Relief washed across his face, and for an instant, I felt bad for making him wait. "You really are hungry, aren't you?" I asked as we walked toward What Came First?

"I am. Last thing I had to eat was with you at Wendy's yesterday."

We were the first in line, and our orders were prepared and out to us with satisfying speed. "Really, Rogan? I could have fixed you something before you left last night, if I had known you weren't going to have dinner." Sitting across from Rogan at a wobbly wooden picnic table, I tore into my scrambled eggs with surprising velocity.

Excellent manners seemed ingrained in Rogan, and though he was evidently on the brink of starvation, he first laid out a paper napkin in his lap, then carefully cut his chicken tenders into manageable bites.

I filled my mouth with fluffy yellow goodness and watched as he folded his hands in his lap and closed his eyes. I sat there awkwardly, my jaw moving slower and slower as I realized he must be praying for his food.

And here I was, tearing into my food like a heathen, my mouth full of scrambled egg and no place to spit it out. Not that I really wanted to spit it out, because I did feel hungry. But I felt like I needed to do something to hide the fact that I clearly hadn't paused to do what he was doing. I was also filling my face with food as he did something spiritual.

Had he done this yesterday, before we ate lunch in the van? Thinking back, I realized he might have. I'd been too busy crushing and then sprinkling crackers into my chili to pay any attention.

Rogan opened his eyes and smiled at me as he picked up his plastic spork.

I clamped a hand over my mouth as if it would hide the mountain of eggs I'd shoved in there, waiting several seconds before resuming my sinful mastication.

Between bites, Rogan spoke, "Getting used to the weirdness of the festival?"

"I think so," I answered honestly. "It felt really weird at first, but being in a forest filled with pirates and fairies is beginning to feel normal, in some bizarre way."

"Pirates and fairies and trolls." He wiggled his eyebrows at me as he took another bite of spork-impaled chicken.

I laughed, relishing the easy companionship I had with him, how comfortable he made me feel. "Yes. And trolls. What would we do without them?"

"Probably have our wings remain entangled on angry tree branches," he said soberly.

"Most likely," I replied. My gaze drifted over at the sudden busyness of the festival. A horde of vendors, cast, and security guys had just come through the back entrance gate. The security guys were always simple to spot, I'd learned over the last few weeks. They were always the ones in red plaid kilts and matching berets, or whatever those flat caps were called. They looked like berets to me.

I watched as they laughed and talked with each another, their familiarity with one another easily recognizable.

Something else, I realized with an abrupt sort of agony, now became easily recognizable.

The endlessly horrifying sensation that my stomach was about to come out through my nose. Frantic, my eyes darted around for a trash can. Spotting one over on the side of the Soup and a Song building, I stood on wobbly legs, ready to run. Once again, I clamped a hand over my mouth as I stumbled toward the can.

Rogan rose, as well, realizing the difficulty I was in. Even as he stood, he wiped his mouth with his napkin and crumbled it onto his plate. Within seconds, he was jogging in my direction.

Why, oh why, had I not taken that prescription pill this morning?

That's the problem with me, I guess. I'm often an idiot in need of rescue.

"Keisha!" a familiar male voice shouted, and I was suddenly emptying my stomach with a horrendous speed. Vomit and bile rushed up my throat and into the can, and my insides shook with pure terror. I fumbled for Rogan, who stood just beside me, pulling napkin after napkin from the dispenser on the Soup and a Song's front counter. Clawing for his attention, I finally caught hold of the fabric of his t-shirt. Intent on getting me something to wipe my face with, I wasn't sure if Rogan had heard the man calling my name.

"Rogan," I sobbed, looking up through blurry eyes. "Help, help me." Pleading for help between bursts of vomiting seemed next to impossible, but it was paramount to get his attention on me.

Pity lined his features as he patted my puke-splattered face. "That's it, that's it, dear, just get it all out and you'll feel better.

Once your stomach settles a bit, I'll go back to your camper and get those pills the doctor gave you yesterday."

He didn't understand.

"Keisha! You stupid bitch, I know you're here!" Vince was closer, his voice nearing us with terrifying intensity.

How had he found me? My hands, which had been gripping the sides of the trash can, now moved of their own accord to cover my belly. Vince didn't know about the baby; he couldn't know.

He wasn't stable. He was violent. I had to get away.

Yet here I was, trapped in the food court, unable to move. The proverbial sitting duck.

"Rogan," I begged once again between heaves. I looked up at him, hoping he would recognize the fear in my face and understand.

Rogan stilled and took two fast steps toward me. I felt his hand on my back, rubbing circles. "Who is that, Keisha?" He threw the wad of filthy napkins he'd been wiping my face with away.

I crouched as far down as I possibly could and still be able to take aim into the trash can. "Vince," I whispered, "Help me, Rogan." Another fountain of liquid misery went into the can. "He doesn't know about the baby. Don't—" I paused as another wave of agony shot through me, "tell him. Not safe."

My stomach began to cramp.

In the van yesterday, I had told him about Vince's alcoholism and the abuse. Those things had been hard for me to say, but now I felt glad I had done it.

Rogan was a smart man. He would put it together quickly.

I hoped.

More than anything else in that moment, I wanted to run. But I knew my shaking legs wouldn't hold me. My bones suddenly had the strength of rotten bananas. Instead, I clutched at Rogan, holding on to my only anchor as I heard Vince's voice the last time he had hit me reverberating in my mind.

"Next time, Keisha..."

And here we were, I thought. At the next time.

In The Presence Of Knowing

I knew in my heart, in my bones, pain was coming.

Through the strange haze of fear in my mind, I found myself admiring Rogan's perfect posture as I slumped against the green metal of the trash can, curled up as small as I could possibly make myself.

"Jason," I heard Rogan say urgently.

From the corner of my eye, red plaid fabric swished.

"Problem, Rogan?" asked another man. Presumably Jason, who wasn't anyone I'd met yet. Though I still hadn't met everyone at Windy Springs, I wouldn't be meeting anyone else if Vince killed me today. The sensation of laughter bubbled up in my chest, and I wondered if this was what hysteria felt like.

"Problem, yes." His voice lowered as he leaned nearer to Jason, and Jason, who was taller than I, bent down to listen.

Their voices blended together, becoming nothing but background noise to me, as I heard Vince call out for me again.

"Goddamn you, Keisha! I know you're here! Get out here where I can see you!"

A sob escaped my lips, so I shoved a fist in my mouth to prevent it from happening again. *Stay quiet, stay still. Don't make him mad. Don't move.*

"You think I wouldn't find you? You can't hide from me!" His voice sounded farther away now. He must have turned down a different path in the forest, taking him in another direction.

People had noticed him, of course. I could hear them talking, wondering who this guy was. "Call security," I heard one woman say loudly.

Red plaid swished past me again, and then Rogan was back at my side, whispering assurances to me. "You know the pub?" he asked, cradling my shoulders in his arm.

The pub? What did he want, a beer? Still, through my panic, I answered with a nod.

"Listen, Keisha."

I nodded again. Really, my skills at nodding were above par, which was great, because at this point, none of the rest of me seemed able to move. "The pub," I repeated in a barely audible whisper.

His arm squeezed against me as he pulled me gently to a standing position. I didn't want to stand. I wanted to melt into the ground, become impossible for anyone to find ever again. I tried to sink back to my position next to the trash can.

"Ah-ah, Keisha. Got to keep moving. We're going to the pub." He pushed me forward, and my legs seemed to propel on their own without my brain doing any sort of work. His arm slunk down so it was around my hips, his fingers digging into my side.

The way we were moving, we could have been running a three-legged race instead of fleeing from my crazy ex-boyfriend.

"The pub," I repeated stupidly. We were going a different way than what I was used to, slipping behind buildings in the food court, waiting behind each one until Rogan had peered out from a corner to be certain the coast was clear.

Sticks and branches tore at my bare legs, and at some point, I lost one of my flip-flops, but we kept running. Something small scurried over my foot, and I barely registered it. The sun had risen higher in the sky, and I could feel sweat running down my back. Which was weird, because I felt cold. Gooseflesh rippled along my arms and legs. My breath hitched in my chest as I stumbled along with Rogan.

Finally, we arrived, slipping into the pub through the back door and ending up in the kitchen. We stopped for a moment and stood together, Rogan's arm still around me, breathing hard. I looked around, noting vaguely the fact that the appliances in the pub kitchen were modern and shiny.

Somewhere in my mind, I'd supposed it would look like the kitchens in period dramas I'd seen on television.

Somewhere in my mind, I remembered Vince was here and was going to hurt me.

Hurt my baby.

"Rogan," I said. Words were failing me. How could I adequately describe my level of utter fear?

I recalled, with sickening detail, the feeling of Vince's fist crashing into my cheek.

The way it had felt to hit the floor, my head bouncing off it at first, like a rag doll.

Stay still. Stay quiet. Don't make him mad. Don't move.

Rogan was talking, and I came back to myself, to the moment. I shook my head. "What?"

"I said, under the pub is the tornado shelter. We're going there. Come on." He pulled at my waist, but I didn't move. He took my hand pulled harder. "Now, Keisha."

I wanted to move, but felt frozen. In my mind, I berated myself. *Move, move, go, go!*

Rogan yanked at me again. "Now!"

Suddenly, I was released from my self-imposed petrified state and stumbled forward, following along as Rogan dragged me toward a large metal door. Down the stairs. Into a dark, cement-floored basement with a variety of boxes, signs, and wench costumes strewn about.

"We are taking care of the situation. You're safe."

I clung to him, hearing myself hyperventilating but unable to stop it.

"Keisha, do you hear me? You're safe. We will not let him near you."

Unable to speak, I nodded my head. Really, I could get a prize for nodding. A nice trophy, maybe.

"You are going to stay right here, and you are not to come up the stairs until I come to get you. Hear me? Do not go with anyone else."

Once again, I started to nod, until his words sank in. *Wait. He's he going to leave me?*

Twisting the fabric of his t-shirt in my fists, I bent down, frantically trying to cling to him any way possible. "No, no, no. Don't leave me," I gasped.

He peeled me off, holding my arms straight at my sides. "Keisha," he spoke firmly. "I have to go. I will take care of this. But you must stay here." His green eyes were serious. Firm.

"But I—?"

"Staying here keeps the baby safe, Keisha," he cut me off. "Wait for me here. I will come back for you."

The baby. Right.

Realizing he would not be swayed, I did the one thing I knew how to do best.

I nodded.

I waited in the basement, alone.

Surely, opening time for the festival had come and gone, and still, Rogan had not come back.

I thought perhaps Layla would come, but she didn't.

The nausea had subsided somewhat.

The cramping had not. I lay on the cold cement floor, my knees curled up to my chest, my arms wrapped around my knees. Wave after wave of pain shot through my abdomen, something akin to menstrual cramps, but worse. Muscle spasms shivered through my lower back.

Lit only by a single dim bulb, the basement of the pub wasn't a friendly place. Shadows lurked on the concrete block walls. So far beneath the ground, I could hear absolutely nothing.

The silence ate at me.

Guilt slithered across my skin.

Vince was here for *me*. My presence had drawn him here. For all I knew, he had a weapon on him, and my friends at the festival could end up hurt.

Layla. Layla could be hurt by Vince.

And so could Rogan. At that thought, the nausea returned for a moment.

I didn't want him harmed, especially not on my account.

My eyes remained on the long staircase. I tried to will Rogan to open the door and come down to me.

The effort, it seemed, was wasted.

Suddenly, a loud crash boomed upstairs in the pub. The heavy footsteps of several different people could be heard. Twice, I heard a shrill scream.

Then another crash, followed by what sounded like a body hitting the floor.

Involuntarily, I winced. I knew what it felt like to slam against a floor that way.

Crawling across the floor, one hand protectively across my belly, I slid behind several tall boxes full of wench costumes and discarded signs. Grasping a wad of polyester fabric in my hand, I dragged a few of the wench waitress costumes across the gap between the two uppermost boxes. Curling up to make myself as small as I possibly could, I stayed still as a statue, my breaths coming slow and ragged.

Men were talking. Doors slammed. The upstairs went silent again.

More time passed. My legs went numb as I remained in my cramped position. Minutes turned to hours.

The door opened, and footsteps thundered down the stairs. Pain blazed through my chest, and I fought to keep control of my mind. Panic was making it next to impossible to think straight.

Please be Rogan, please be Rogan, please, please.

"Keisha?" a female voice called me. "Are you down here, Keisha?"

It was Layla. Disappointment crashed through me, and on top of my fear of Vince, I felt a stab of disloyalty.

I had so badly wanted it to be Rogan coming for me.

Layla had been my best friend for years… the one who'd taken me in when I had nobody else. Had given me a job, a home, and a support system.

I should have wanted her to come to my rescue.

"Keisha? Come on, it's okay. Vince has been—taken care of. It's safe."

I could hear her fast, excited breathing as she waited for my response. Opening my mouth to call back to her, I found the words frozen in my throat. I knew I could trust Layla, but still, I remembered Rogan's words when he told me not to go with anyone else.

This was ridiculous. I knew it as well as I knew my own name.

Yet, I remained still and quiet, then eventually, Layla gave up and went back up the stairs.

In my protective, make-shift fort, I sat for what seemed like an eternity before I once again, heard footsteps descending the stairs.

The footsteps wandered the basement, coming closer and closer to me. I held my breath for as long as I could, but finally blew out a breath slowly, quietly.

Through a crack between the cardboard boxes I was hiding behind, I could see a pair of hairy, muscular legs beneath well-worn cargo shorts.

Rogan.

Relief washed through me in waves, both because he was here, safe and, I assumed, whole, and also because his presence meant the threat of Vince was gone. My breath shuddered, and I uttered a low, keening wail, reaching up through the wench costumes that had hidden me.

Instantly, he was next to me, his arms wrapping sturdily around me, whispering in my ear, "Sshh, sshh, sshh. It's over, it's over. You're safe. It's okay, sweetheart."

With my head against his chest, I listened to the steady beating of his heart. It was calming to me, that reliable *thump-thump, thump-thump.*

It took me a second to work the words up into my throat, and when I did, they were barely audible, "He's gone?" The idea that Vince had even been there to begin with had been stunning. How had he found me?

With his chin against my head, I felt Rogan nod. "Vince is gone. He's been… taken care of. You are perfectly safe. Are you ready to stand up?"

Rogan helped me to stand, though my legs were still wobbly and cramped from their forced, awkward position. The pains through my abdomen had ceased, however, and for this, I felt immensely grateful. I picked at my clothes, situating myself, stalling for time. I knew I could trust him, but a little seed of doubt still worried the back of my mind. "You're—you're sure he's gone?" I needed to hear it, at least once more. I had thought before that I was rid of Vince, but look what had just happened. Peering down, I stared hard into Rogan's eyes.

"I'm sure, Keisha. I promise."

His sweet, honest face told me I could believe him. "Layla came." I still felt ashamed for not reaching out to her when she'd stood on the stairs, calling for me.

"I know. But you did right, waiting for me." His hand reached up to caress my cheek. "The festival owner decided to close us down for the day, until we get everyone calmed down and the grounds cleaned up. It's a bit of a mess up there."

Guilt, once again, pricked at me. It was my fault the festival had to close; people would lose money because of me. "I'm sorry."

Grasping my chin in his hand, Rogan tilted my head downward. "Keisha, listen to me. This situation is *not* your fault. You are the victim, here. And we are your friends. We *want* to help keep you and the baby safe."

In that instant, I felt a sense of belonging, of *rightness,* I had never felt before. I had friends here. Some of these people I had barely spoken to beyond a 'good morning' wave as I carried in boxes to set up the shop, but they had just fought for me. There was so much in my soul, so many emotions I wanted to express, but the words just tumbled around in my head like clothes in a laundromat dryer.

I found two of them and latched on tight. Brushing my hand across Rogan's stubble-lined head, I said, "Thank you."

The stain of the fight with Vince was everywhere.

Obviously, he had not backed down easily. Wooden picnic tables as well as the tables that resembled gigantic wooden thread spools in the food court had been overturned. Walking through the aftermath of the morning with Rogan and Layla, my abdominal muscles repeatedly seized with angst. Small bushes had been ripped out along some places on the paths.

Several kilt-clad security guards stopped to offer me words of encouragement and solidarity.

Grok and Bork, the Hot Gnome Brothers, each took turns enveloping me in a lung-crushing hug.

We stopped at On a Wing and a Prayer, where the patchwork-covered tables had been knocked over, and Layla's beautiful, intricate fairy wings lay scattered in the dirt. For a moment, the three of us stood there, frozen to our spots, taking in the wreckage.

Finally, I spoke, "I'm so sorry, Lay." Everywhere I went, misery followed. "I will help you fix them. I'll make more. Take my pay to buy more supplies!" It wasn't enough. There was no way I could ever make this right. Clearing my throat, I said, "Maybe I should go back to your house to stay for a while, Lay. I don't want anyone else to get hurt because of me."

Layla turned to me, her eyes wide. "No, Keisha. You are staying right here, with us. Where you belong. Rennies stick together. It's the rule. Besides, you're my best friend, and I'm not letting you go anywhere."

She didn't understand. Everything with Vince had been my fault. Hadn't he told me that, over and over? Today was no exception. Everyone at Windy Springs had been put in danger this morning because of me. Layla's wings were ruined, Rogan's face looked like he'd been the recipient of several harsh blows, and two of the security guards had been hurt. The burden of my role in this situation shook me to my core.

Rogan took my hand in his and squeezed. "*We* aren't letting you go anywhere. Just put that thought out of your head, Keisha. You are wanted here. You belong. If someone comes after one of us, they come after us all."

Layla was the first to make a move. With a deep sigh, she bent down to begin retrieving the bronze remnants of weeks of hard work, collecting each set of wings carefully in her arms.

Her movement jolted us both into action, as Rogan and I began picking up wings from the dirt path surrounding On a Wing and a Prayer. As he worked, Rogan whistled some bawdy pirate tune I'd heard at least a hundred times from the band that played on the stage near the food court every afternoon, the Rowdy Rennies.

Around us, conversations between vendors, cast, and security guards hummed along. People were working together to fix the mess my presence had caused. As I leaned down to pick up another set of trampled wings and dust them off, Rogan's voice rumbled across the lane, "Layla."

He sounded... I wasn't sure. Not angry, but serious. Concerned, perhaps.

I lifted my head and saw them both heading toward me. My stomach began to cramp again, and I flung an arm over my middle and pressed against it. Layla and Rogan together shoved me behind a thick-trunked tree and stood in front of me.

"What...?" I started to ask what on earth was going on, but Rogan turned his face to me quickly, one finger over his pressed lips, shaking his head.

I shut up. They were obviously trying to hide me from someone, and the only person I could imagine hiding from was Vince. But Rogan had promised me they had gotten Vince to leave, so who were we hiding from?

Silent, I peeked out between Rogan and Layla's shoulders as they stood side-by-side in front of me. The only person coming down the lane was Cordelia, the blue-haired witch lady. Wearing a long, silver-blue gown with enormous bell-shaped sleeves, she walked slowly along, stabbing at the dirt path with her ornately carved wooden staff. Nearby vendors turned away from her, busying themselves with straightening their shelves and merchandise. The closer she came, the more my stomach cramped. She had almost walked past our little group that was huddled against the tree, when she suddenly spun and turned toward us. One gnarled hand lifted in painfully slow motion, and she pointed a wrinkled finger in our direction.

A sickening, satisfied smile spread across her face.

I held my breath, as if doing so might make us invisible. Unable to break my gaze, I continued to peer through the tiny space between Rogan and Layla's shoulders.

After a few seconds, Cordelia resumed her walk, and the usual chatter returned to our lane as shopkeepers went back to their normal activities. Rogan and Layla moved forward, back to On a Wing and a Prayer, as though the last several minutes had been perfectly typical.

I followed them. "What was that about?" I demanded.

They met each other's eyes, but remained silent.

Frustrated, I kept pushing. "Seriously, guys, what is with that lady? Does she have some kind of problem with me?"

Layla spoke first, "Cordelia can be… dangerous." It seemed obvious she was choosing her words carefully, deciding what knowledge I was worthy of getting. "I've told you before, stay away from her."

"Dangerous?" I echoed. She had to be at least in her mid-sixties. How dangerous could one borderline-elderly blue-haired woman be? "What's she going to do, put a spell on me?" I joked.

Neither of them laughed or even cracked a smile. Rogan and Layla did that irritating thing where they locked eyes for a second before either one of them talked to me.

Rogan's jaw clenched and he shut his eyes briefly as he pinched the bridge of his nose. There were scratches on his face from the altercation this morning with Vince, as well as a big bruise crawling up one side of his face. When he rubbed his hands across his eyes, I noted the scrapes across his knuckles.

Vince had really put up a fight. I shivered, despite the heat of midday.

With a heavy sigh, Rogan opened his eyes and said, "Keisha, I need for you to trust me on this." His hand fluttered toward Layla and back to himself. "Trust us. Cordelia is not someone you need to be around. Stay away from her. She is, as Layla said, dangerous."

An icy finger of dread crept up my spine. I suddenly thought of all the times my stomach had cramped when I'd been anywhere near her. And with blazing clarity, I recalled the day I'd gotten sick and Pirate Jack had ridden with me to the emergency room. Just prior to my collapse, I'd seen Cordelia in the lane, perusing racks of merchandise. New and hoping to make friends at Windy Springs, I had smiled and waved at her. She had not returned my greeting in the least, I remembered now.

Shortly after this, the pain came.

It seemed ridiculous to think she'd had anything to do with my illness and collapse that day. I didn't actually believe in witches and fairies along with all the other things people at the festival pretended to be.

But Rogan and Layla had such serious looks on their faces, I knew something wasn't right with that woman, so I slowly nodded in compliance. "I'll stay away from her. No worries."

Quietly, we returned to our task of picking up the ruined wings.

CHAPTER TEN

It was the first night since I'd come to Windy Springs that I finally went to the community pot luck dinner at the end of the day. I'd developed a routine of zipping through just as the food was set out, piling it on my plate, and slipping out to the camper to eat in silence, book in hand. Conversing with a large group of people I barely knew made me feel as though ants were crawling on my skin. After acting cheerful and gregarious with a fake British accent all day long, I craved time alone, away from even my best friend. The exceptionally social nature of the festival was something I often found exhausting.

But tonight, I got my plate of food and slid onto a stool at one of the big wooden tables shaped like an enormous spool, right next to Layla and Jack. Though the festival had remained closed for the day after the altercation with Vince that morning, everyone seemed in high spirits, and so far, I hadn't run into anyone who had given me any crap about Vince showing up there in search of me.

I suddenly realized I felt this strange feeling, of not having to constantly be on the defensive or apologetic.

"So," I began as I crushed crackers into my chili bread bowl, "what did the owner tell people when they arrived this morning? Just that the festival was closed?" I hoped anyone who'd been turned away today would come back tomorrow, so none of the vendors lost out on more business on my behalf.

Layla laughed. "Oh, no." She took a sip of her piping hot coffee. "Dashiel made a whole detailed story up about how some of the water pipes in the food court had burst and the lanes were flooded."

"And people believed that?" It didn't sound believable to my ears, but maybe because I was here and knew the real reason behind the closure. I'd developed a quiet rhythm, taking a bite, chewing, pretending to look thoughtfully around while I really scanned the area for Vince. Despite the reassurances of everyone at Windy Springs, I still felt on edge, like he could be hiding behind a building, just waiting to jump out and grab me. After checking the periphery of my surroundings once more, I forced myself to focus on Jack's words.

"People will often accept the world as it is presented to them, without question." He didn't look at me as he talked, just slathered ketchup onto his slab of chicken-on-a-stake and took a messy bite. "It helps that Dad's such an imposing figure. Folks tend not to argue with him." This time, he did look up at me, grinning with ketchup all over his lips.

"Is he? I haven't had the chance to meet him yet." I yanked several paper napkins from the container and handed them to Jack. "I should thank him."

"He'll be around sometime during the meal. Trust me, you can't miss him." Layla rolled her eyes and bit her lip.

"He's kind of different," Jack added.

At this, I laughed. "Isn't just about everyone here kind of different?"

"Just wait. You'll see what I mean. When he gets here, I'll introduce you." She waved to someone behind me. "Oh, hey, Gibble! Sit with us!"

Rogan sidled up next to me and hopped onto a stool. His feet dangled mid-air, his legs too short to reach the ground.

Wise to his praying game, I didn't take another bite until after he'd closed his eyes for a few seconds.

Then he tore into his cheeseburger like a man on a mission, pausing every few seconds to wipe crumbs from his face. "Did you take your pill, Keisha?" Rogan asked me, patting my knee as if I were a child.

"Yes, Mom," I replied, both grateful and mildly irritated. On the one hand, I disliked being treated like a little kid. On the other, it was nice, for a change, to have someone else looking out for my welfare.

"Good girl," he said, grinning at me.

Rogan really did have the nicest smile, when he didn't have those awful troll teeth in. His actual teeth were crooked, but they gave him a cheery, rakish appearance when he grinned.

"Dad!" Jack called.

I looked up, expecting to see someone who resembled Pirate Jack on some level, and in this vein, I was seriously disappointed. Jack's father was taller, broader, and blonder than Jack would ever be. A hot tingle shot from between my legs to my chest. I sat up taller, patting my frizzy black hair.

Hello, Jack's daddy.

If Jack played a pirate, then his father must've been the pirate king. Long, heavy blond dreadlocks hung over his shoulders, bits of string, beads, and other small shiny items tied into them at random. Thick black eyeliner shadowed his eyelids and just below his big blue eyes. His puffy white shirt had a slit in the center nearly down to his navel, and a mass of fuzzy blonde curls was visible inside it. He plopped down on a stool next to his son and grinned at us. His smile was blindingly shiny.

Most of his teeth were covered in sparkling gold caps.

He pointed at me, and I saw that each finger on his hand was sporting a large gaudy ring. Even his thumbs and pinkies.

"Huzzah!" he shouted, pounding the table. His voice was as enormous as he was. "You must be the infamous Keisha."

Our plates and cups bounced against the wood.

I waved. "Infamous Keisha. That's me. And you must be Dash—"

Layla kicked me under the table. *Hard.* Cupping her hand across the lower part of her face, she leaned in to me and whispered, "You have to call him Captain."

What?

"What?" I hissed at her.

"Call him Captain," she repeated, widening her eyes and wiggling her brows.

Unsure if I was in the midst of some elaborate prank, I went along with it. If everyone else knew and I didn't do it, I didn't want to get laughed at.

The day had been difficult enough already.

"Captain Dashiel," I amended, though I could hear a question in my tone. If Layla had been screwing around and made a laughingstock of me, I was going to do something to get back at her. Something really mean.

Maybe I would hide all her boxes of baby wipes.

"Oh now, little lady, don't be so formal," he boomed, leaning across the table to plant a kiss on my hand.

Layla *had* been screwing with me. Just wait until I found her stash of baby wipes. I would make her *cry.*

"Call me Captain Dash," he continued. "I hear the boys took care of that little issue of yours this morning."

Took care of that little issue. Thinking about it, everyone I'd spoken to about Vince since I came up from the storm shelter under the pub had said something similar to me. That he had been *taken care of.*

What did this mean? Initially, I'd simply been grateful he was gone and apparently, no longer a threat. Had he been arrested? Put in the hospital? Surely, this merry band of pirates, trolls, and kilted guards hadn't actually—murdered my ex-boyfriend, had they?

I swallowed hard around the lump which abruptly formed in my throat and my welcoming smile wavered. "I guess so. I wanted to thank you, um, Captain Dash, for closing the festival today until it was taken care of." When in Rome, I guess. We could speak in euphemisms all day long, but I would have to eventually ask what it meant. "I'm so sorry if I've caused you to lose out on business today."

Narrowing his big blue eyes, he shot me a questioning look. "Little lady, as I understand it, you were the victim in this situation." His large, ring-laden fingers steepled together, his elbows on the wooden table. Captain Dash shook his head. "You don't apologize for being a victim of attack."

There was no doubt Dashiel was heart-meltingly handsome, but if he called me *little lady* one more time, I thought I might scream. "All right, then, Captain Dash. Still, please accept my thanks."

He made a clicking sound with his tongue and pointed at me once again. "No problem at all, little lady." And then he chin-chucked me. He actually did. "You're knowing, right?"

Knowing? "Actually, my name's Keisha." Hadn't he already said my name? Maybe he'd already been hitting the mead. A lot of it.

"Dad," Jack said, as he swatted at his father's arm. "Hush. She isn't."

Beside me, Rogan made an indeterminate sound in his throat, something like a cross between a cough and a laugh.

She isn't. Isn't what?

"Right. Keisha. That chili good? Because this pirate is just about hungry enough to eat a sea horse."

"Oh, it's delicious," I replied as I brought another bite up to my lips. Maybe if I just concentrated on eating, kept my eyes down, Captain Dash would lose interest in me.

"Great!" he boomed as he leaned over the table and snatched my chili bread bowl. "I need a spoon for this," he mumbled as he stood and wandered away, presumably in search of a plastic utensil.

I looked over at Layla. "Did that just happen?" I asked, still holding my spoon in the air.

Jack had the decency to look embarrassed. "Sorry. We should have warned you better. My dad's a bit eccentric."

"He's also a thief." I licked the last few remnants of my wonderful chili from my white plastic spoon. "What kind of person steals chili from a pregnant woman?"

"A pirate," Jack deadpanned. "Don't worry, Keisha. I'll get you another bowl of chili."

Dusk had fallen, the community supper had been put away, and Rogan was walking with me back to the camper.

"Thank you again, for today, Rogan. You kept me safe, and I am so grateful for what you did."

Rogan coughed and cleared his throat, looking away. He was obviously uncomfortable with the attention. "That's what friends do for each other," he replied.

"We've got some antibiotic ointment in the camper, if you want to come in. For the scrapes. On your face, you know?"

Gingerly, he patted his face. "I did get a little banged up, didn't I? I guess it will add to my character tomorrow."

We stopped, and I opened the metal door. "Come in. Let me help take care of you for a change."

Rogan obediently followed me in, barely leaving either of us room to turn around in the tiny space.

"Here, sit on my bed," I said, indicating the horrible orange plaid couch. Grabbing the antibiotic ointment from the small cabinet above the sink and a wash cloth I ran under the faucet for a second, I turned back to my task. Rogan winced slightly as I cleaned his wounds. "We should have done this earlier," I lamented. "I should have thought."

"Nothing that won't heal up on its own, I don't think," he replied, jerking back a bit as I dabbed ointment on a particularly nasty scrape along the bruise on his face. "Ouch. Sorry."

"Big bruise there. It'll be tender for several days yet," I said, remembering as the words tumbled out how much the bruise Vince had left on my own face had hurt, lasting several very painful days.

"Not the first time I've had a run-in with a bad guy, you know, Keisha," he said wryly. "I'm a big boy. I could do this myself."

"I'm sure you could. There, I'm finished. Should I kiss it and make it all better?" I knew as soon as the words left my mouth it was the wrong thing to say. To say the moment became awkward would be a major understatement. I paused, unsure what to say that could retract the question.

Sudden heat wavered in the air between us.

Pink stained Rogan's cheeks, and I was sure, my own as well.

"I suppose you could," he said, his voice low and husky. His hands encircled my wrists, pulling me down toward him. "If you want to."

Layla was off in Pirate Jack's black trailer, having fun and probably something else. She wouldn't be back for a while yet. It was just the two of us. I waited a beat, working to hurriedly sort through my emotions regarding Rogan. First, he had been the funny little troll guy. Then he had become a dependable friend.

Now— now what was he to me? My rescuer?

No, I decided. I didn't view him as a savior of any kind. Yet, I was quickly beginning to think of him as more than a friend.

The day had been highly charged with a vast myriad of feelings and emotions. Keeping my eyes open and fixed on Rogan's, I leaned in slowly, planting a kiss on the bruise that lined the side of his face.

It wasn't a little peck on the cheek. I lingered there, breathing in the scent of him. He smelled of the woods and of sweat. My hands were resting on his shoulders, and I squeezed them briefly as I kissed each scrape on his face. A bit of antibiotic ointment stuck to my lips. I didn't pause to wipe it off.

Rogan sat perfectly straight and still as I did this, breathing steadily, if a little ragged, his hands flat on his knees. He closed his eyes as I kissed him, and I was struck again by how long his eyelashes were. They curled up at the ends; I half-envied him for how pretty they were.

Releasing his shoulders, I picked up his right hand, tenderly dropping a kiss on each knuckle before moving to do the same thing on his left hand.

By now, his breath was hitching every now and again, though his posture remained perfectly straight. "Keisha," he mumbled my name. His free hand came up to touch my hair, gripping it in his fist. "Keisha," he moaned again.

Pausing at the last knuckle, I kept my lips pressed to his skin for several seconds. I didn't want to break the connection we had in this moment. It'd been so long since I had felt truly, physically connected to another human being this way, and I wasn't prepared to let it go. When I finally did release him and straighten up, he seemed hesitant to let me go, and the hand he'd tangled in my hair slid reluctantly down, trailing my neck, shoulder, and arm.

After this type of physical exchange, standing there staring into his beautiful green eyes was too much for me. Too awkward. Too emotional. Breaking eye contact with Rogan, I plopped down beside him on the ugly plaid couch.

With his palms up, resting on his thighs, Rogan stared silently at his hands.

His lack of response shook me. I wasn't sure what I'd been thinking or feeling when I had started kissing him; I just knew it felt like the right thing to do. The necessary thing. I still felt that way, but his silence was undoing me. "Rogan?" I could hear the shakiness in my voice as I spoke his name. "Are you upset?"

He took a deep, shuddering breath. "No." His voice came out low, rumbly.

I waited, but he offered no further indication of how he was feeling. "Say something. Please."

Setting his hand on my thigh, he turned to me, his expression serious. "Keisha. Where do you see this going? See *us* going?"

The truth was, I hadn't thought that far ahead. My actions had been in the moment, born of a need to physically connect with him, coupled with a sense of gratitude for his actions earlier in the day. It wasn't that I felt indebted to Rogan; it was more about the fact I saw the way he cared for me, that in an instant, he would put aside his own wants and even his safety to make sure I was okay. I found a certain safety in his presence, and in this safety, I was finding, there was room for a spark of desire.

I was honest in my reply. "I'm not sure." Right that second, I felt alive with passion, but I wasn't sure if it was from pregnancy hormones, an adrenaline rush from the excitement of the day, or pure, simple attraction to the man beside me.

I'd been borderline invisible in high school, floating through halls and classes untouched by bullies but bereft of the attention of close friends, as well. Getting asked out on a date wasn't the sort of thing that happened to girls like me; quiet, bookish girls uninvolved in sports or popular activities. There had been a handful of first and sometimes second dates in my early adult years, but none that led to anything beyond, until I had met Vince. And though my love for him had been real, I could look back now and see what a complete train wreck our relationship had been from the start. He'd been drowning in his addiction since the beginning, and I had been little more than a slowly deflating life raft, losing myself as I kept trying to rescue him.

Rogan was different. Quietly confident in himself, he was steady. Reliable. Funny. And something else. Something that made me want to get to know him, all of him, beyond the confines of friendship. But I couldn't only think about the things I wanted, not anymore. There was someone else involved. I finally spoke. "There's the baby." Rogan was, as far as I was aware, unattached. Perhaps he wasn't interested in the prospect of a ready-made family.

"There's the baby," he agreed. "But that changes nothing from where I sit, Keisha."

It changed a lot from where I sat. It was changing my entire life.

Some days, I felt as though I was falling through the air, desperately trying and failing to find something sturdy to hold on to.

I covered his hand on my thigh with my own. "I don't want to rush."

Rogan snorted. "Sweetheart, I haven't been with a woman in five years. I'm not the rushing sort."

"We don't have to decide today, right? We can be friends and keep moving forward just to see where this goes." Couldn't we? Or would failing to label whatever it was between cause the light to die out?

Nodding, Rogan made a little noise of agreement. "We can do that. But Keisha, you need to understand that if we are going to go slow with this – and I agree with you that we should – I'm not playing games here. I told you before, I don't give myself away lightly. If I'm in, I'm in one hundred percent. I can't, I won't, dangle along forever on the brink of a relationship."

"Could you see us together, though, Rogan?" I needed to know if the possibility was just in my imagination.

Jack and Layla were outside the camper, talking. Their voices wafted in through the thin metal door. Then a soft thud sounded against the outside.

I resisted the urge to roll my eyes. They were probably making out…Again.

He rose abruptly, facing me, and the place where his hand had been on my thigh felt empty and cold. With his thumb, he trailed along the side of my face, stopping at my chin. "I could, Keisha. I've been seeing us together since I first rescued you from the angry tree branch. But I would rather have your true and dedicated friendship than a half-hearted relationship. I'll wait while you decide." He walked toward the door. "See you tomorrow, Keisha."

I wanted to say something, anything, to make him stay. I wanted to go to him, drag him back to the stupid orange plaid couch, and tell him I needed him to hold me, that I needed to rest in his strong arms, just for tonight.

I wanted to ask him what they'd done with Vince, what "taken care of" meant.

I wanted to ask him a lot of things. The words sat on my tongue, ready to be spoken, but my mouth remained shut.

Instead, I sat still and silent on the couch as he walked out the door.

CHAPTER ELEVEN

June 2010

Weeks had passed, and much as May had been, June in the forest was abnormally warm. My regular jean shorts had started to become tight on me, and I was grudgingly thankful for Layla's foresight in making my fairy tutus with elastic waists.

Soon enough, I'd need to start buying bigger clothes. Layla didn't pay me a lot, but without many bills of my own to pay, I'd saved enough to buy a few things. I'd just needed to take a trip into town, but kept putting it off because though I didn't want to admit it out loud, I felt safer staying within the confines of Windy Springs.

I still didn't know what had become of Vince. I wasn't sure I wanted to ask.

Sometimes answers only created more problems.

The festival had been hopping with patrons for hours, and I was looking forward to break time. I rubbed my belly, saliva pooling in my mouth at the thought of another bowl of chili. Rogan had taken to having his lunch break at the same time as me, so we often sat together in the food court, enjoying each other's company. My feet ached from standing for so many hours without a break. Another half an hour and it would be break time. It would be 'hanging out with Rogan' time. I grinned at the thought of it.

We'd grown closer over the last several weeks, though we had yet to make a decision about the direction our relationship was headed. Still, it was nice just being together. We did a lot of talking.

The more I knew about Rogan, the more time I wanted to spend with him.

As if summoned by my thoughts, Rogan appeared at On a Wing and a Prayer, his terrible false teeth sticking up from his lower lip. "Break time!"

"Almost. Layla's gone for lunch at the moment, so I have to wait for her to get back." Every other day during the festival, we took turns going to lunch first.

The Zofran had helped with the morning sickness, and lately I rarely even felt the waves of nausea that had been so frequent earlier in my pregnancy. As I entered my second trimester, I also felt much less exhausted all the time. I hoped the remainder of my gestation would be as pleasant.

Rogan offered a quick hug. "All right. Be back in a few." Off he went, playing his part, drawing children and the occasional adult patron into his act. Laughter rang out, following him down the lane.

Several minutes later, Layla returned and I looked around hopefully for Rogan.

"Looking for Gibble?" she asked. "I saw him around the corner just a few minutes ago."

"Rogan," I corrected for the umpteenth time. I understood that during festival hours we were supposed to call cast by their character names, but between the two of us, I wanted her to call him by his real name. I felt like she didn't want to acknowledge he was anything more than the humorous troll. "His name is Rogan."

He'd grown to be important to me, and a big part of my life. I didn't want Layla to view Rogan as some kind of joke.

"Right. I keep forgetting," she said, waving a hand dismissively in the air. She dragged another box of bronze wings from inside the hut to replace those that had been sold. "Anyway, you can go ahead to lunch if you want."

"I'll wait until he gets here." A woman dressed as a belly dancer handed me a set of wings and I rang them up. After wrapping them carefully in bubble wrap and sliding them into a bag, I smiled brightly. "G'day, lash, and many thanks for shopping at On a Wing and a Prayer!" That was something else that had changed about me over the month and a half I'd been working with Layla: Talking weird with the bad accent was getting easier for me.

Layla glanced at me, her eyes narrowing quizzically.

"What?" I asked, turning my palms upward and shrugging.

"Nothing," she said, as she went back to her task.

Rogan's hand settled on the small of my back, just below my own set of wings. "Ready?"

He had snuck up on me again, but I didn't mind. Spinning, so that we were face to face, I smiled. "Sure am," I responded. To Layla, I said, "Lay, we're going to lunch, okay?"

She was with a patron, but waved me off.

As we waited in line at a Soup and a Song, the Rapunzel girl kept belting out her music above us, customer after costumer stomped away angrily. We approached, and the clearly overworked, sweaty wench that worked the front counter looked like she was about to weep.

Brushing a wayward strand of blonde hair from her face, she explained they had run out of hamburger, and therefore had no chili for the bread bowls. An unusually high volume of chili orders over the weekend had caused them to run out of meat.

"We still have chowder in a bread bowl, though, and broccoli cheese," she offered.

That sounded terrible to me, and the expression on my face must have reflected my reaction.

Speaking to the wench, Rogan asked, "If I run into town and buy more hamburger, would you make my fuchsia fairy friend here a bowl of chili?" She looked about to protest, but Rogan held up a hand before continuing, "I'll pay for the meat and double for the chili. And I'll give you a good tip."

"Rogan," I said, pinching his mud-splattered sleeve. "You don't have to do that."

"I know I don't have to, but I would like to." He turned to the wench. "Well?"

She looked nervously over her shoulder before replying, "Listen, the boss isn't here at the moment, but if you make it quick, I'll do it. I'll start the chili now, so don't take too long. A good tip, right?"

Though it often felt as though we were far from civilization, in reality the town was less than ten minutes away. Still, though. Ten minutes there, ten minutes back, plus time to cook the meat, would take our entire lunch break.

"I don't think we have the time, Rogan," I insisted. "I don't want you to get in trouble."

Rogan rolled his eyes. "You let Layla know what's going on and I'm sure she'll be fine with you taking a few extra minutes for lunch. My boss is Captain Dash, and I'll tell him I'm rescuing a distressing damsel. I mean, a damsel in distress." He winked at me. "He's all for rescuing damsels."

I really *did* want that chili. I decided, in the interest of the baby, I would go along with it.

In the passenger seat of Rogan's SUV, I felt as though we were making a prison break. Not that I viewed Windy Springs Renaissance Festival as a prison. I just felt like we were doing something forbidden as we sped out of the parking lot and onto the road toward town. The sensation left me giddy.

"I'm just coming along because you're doing this for me. I'm not going into the store dressed as a fairy."

Rogan quirked his brow. "Because it's not at all humiliating to be dressed as a muddy troll, alone, buying a package of hamburger."

"At least you don't have your teeth in anymore." He'd taken them out before we left the festival. "And you've got your shoes on, so you aren't going in barefoot," I added helpfully. "You look fine."

"Yeah, sure. I'm certain the cashier will think I look just fine." He laughed as he turned down the street the small grocery store was on.

"Windy Springs has been going here a long time. I'm sure they've had pirates and trolls come in at least on occasion to buy things. They won't think anything of it."

"Pirates and trolls, but not fairies, huh?"

"Not this fairy, anyway," I said, staring out the window as we drove through the little town. It was more like a village, really. I smoothed the tulle of my tutu down against my legs. We turned into the lot and Rogan parked.

"I'll be back in a minute. Don't go anywhere," he said.

"Ha-ha. You're funny," I replied. "Trust me, I'm not going anywhere." I watched as he strode into the store, doing a half bow any time someone stopped to stare at him. I had no doubt, if he'd been wearing a hat, he would have doffed it each time.

He was back faster than I had anticipated, handing me the bag containing the package of hamburger as he slid into his seat.

"What did Captain Dash say when you told him what you were doing?" I asked. Since the day he'd stolen my food, I hadn't had much interaction with the man. I knew he was pretty well always on the faire grounds during the weekends, but he spent most of his time in his office, which was located near the rear of the faire, situated inside an enormous wooden pirate ship.

"He said, Gibble, always take good care of that little lady. Go forth and save your damsel!"

I laughed outright at Rogan's imitation of the festival owner. "He did not say that."

"He did. Exactly that."

"Jack said he was eccentric, but I think he's more like a chronic drunk." A drop-dead gorgeous chronic drunk, I thought, but saw no reason to mention that to Rogan.

Rogan shook his head. "Nah, the Captain rarely drinks, actually. That's all him. All year long."

"All year long, what?"

"All year long, he dresses and talks that way."

"Even when the festival isn't going?"

"Even then." Rogan pointed at the side of his head and made a slow, circling motion, indicating what he thought of Captain Dash's mental status. "But a heart of gold, really. He's a good man."

"I'm sure," I said, for lack of anything better to say.

"Oh shit," Rogan muttered, slowing the vehicle and pulling off to the side of the road.

"What? What is it?" A flat tire? Was an ambulance coming behind us? I peered in my side mirror to see.

"Cops." He rubbed at his eyes, smearing more mud onto his face. "I know I wasn't speeding."

The wailing of the siren rose and fell in waves behind us, and though I knew we hadn't done anything wrong, my bones still trembled with panic. Fight or flight response activated. I had a fleeting vision of opening the SUV door and running down the road.

"Could you open the glove box and give me the insurance and registration proofs there, please, Keisha?" Rogan asked me with a heavy sigh.

He rolled down his window as the officer approached, holding tightly to his license and the proofs I had given him.

"Any idea why I pulled you over this afternoon?" asked the officer as he flipped open a small pad and began scribbling on it. When he looked up and into the vehicle at us, his mouth dropped open and he stood there, staring.

The fight or flight sensation disappeared, replaced entirely by complete and utter humiliation.

I wondered what the police officer – who looked like he was all of sixteen – was thinking as he took in the scene before him. He'd pulled over a vehicle for a routine traffic stop, and found two adults dressed like fairytale creatures in the front seat. And

Rogan… Rogan was not only dressed in his troll costume, he was also covered in mud.

Rogan spoke soberly. "No officer, I don't. I know I wasn't speeding. Is there another problem?" He was sitting up as straight and as tall as possible, which admittedly, wasn't all that tall.

Officer Baby Face seemed to recover his power of speech. "You, uh, you've got a taillight out, right side." Staring intently at us, he continued, "I need to see your license, registration, and insurance."

"Yes sir," Rogan responded, handing his information out the window.

As we waited for Officer Baby Face to check to see if Rogan was a serial killer or something equally nefarious, Rogan whistled, drumming his hands against his thighs.

For the first time, I wondered if his whistling started up during times when he felt nervous. I made a mental note to pay more attention to what was going on when he started up his tunes.

Footsteps approached, and the officer leaned in toward Rogan, handing back his license and other proofs. "Looks like your record is clean, Mr. O'Connor, so I'm not going to give you a ticket today, as long as you promise to get that light fixed."

"Yes sir," Rogan said again, handing the paper squares back to me. There was a low undercurrent of vibration in his tone, as though he was barely able to restrain himself from losing control.

The officer hesitated, remaining near the window. "Mr. O'Connor, can I ask where you and your companion are heading today?"

"Church service, officer," Rogan replied with a straight face.

I laugh-coughed, slapping a hand over my mouth to stop the sound that resembled the barking of a sick seal.

"All right, then," he said, "you two have a good day."

By the time we had pulled away and were once again on the road that led back to Windy Springs, both of us were roaring with laughter.

That was the thing about Rogan. He could always make me laugh, something I realized I'd been sadly lacking in my life.

When I finally got my chili bread bowl from Soup and a Song, I decided it was the best bowl of chili I had ever eaten.

August 2010

Rogan insisted on going with me to every doctor appointment I had, even on days when Layla was free to ride along. I sometimes acted put out about his overprotective attitude, but secretly was grateful. There was always a niggling worry in the back of my mind that Vince would show up again. I felt safer, having Rogan with me.

Though several weeks had passed since the day Vince had shown up at Windy Springs and caused such an uproar, and I had subsequently brought up the possibility of taking our relationship beyond friendship, Rogan and I had not yet talked of it again.

Not any of it. Not Vince. Not me kissing Rogan on the plaid couch in the camper. We were carrying on our relationship, such as it was, in some permanent stage of limbo, more than friends and not quite lovers.

Rogan had offered to drive this time, and as we sailed down the expressway on our way to my appointment, we chatted aimlessly about light, superficial topics, skating the surface of all the things we needed to discuss.

Skating the surface wasn't moving us in any direction, though, and as I watched vehicles on either side passing by us – because Rogan refused to drive even one mile over the speed limit – I came to a decision. I cleared my throat and spoke, "Rogan," I began. "I think there are some things we need to talk about." We had another forty-five minutes until we arrived at my appointment. Enough time to get at least some of what we'd been avoiding talking about out.

Eyes on the road, he replied, "All right. Shoot."

"Can we talk about Vince?" Might as well get the biggest elephant out of the room. Or the SUV, as it were.

"No." I could see the muscles in his jaw clenching, his grip on the steering wheel getting more and more tight. His knuckles were blanching.

"Really?" I hadn't expected an outright refusal.

Releasing a slow breath, he amended, "Not right now, Keisha. Eventually, perhaps."

Weird, but not the outright refusal I had first understood. "I think I've been pretty patient. Is there a particular reason you won't talk to me about him?" Actually, *nobody* at Windy Springs had ever mentioned Vince to me again, after that terrible day.

"Yes, you've been patient. Yes, there is a particular reason. No, I'm not changing my mind. Next question."

I swallowed hard. Twisted my fingers on my lap. "It's been a long time since we've talked about—about our relationship, Rogan. I'd like to revisit that."

"We can do that." Eyes still steadfastly on the road, hands gripping the wheel, he certainly wasn't making it easy to get the conversation rolling.

Waiting a beat, I considered exactly what it was I wanted to say. Best to say it straight out. I'd spent many nights tossing and turning on my stupid plaid couch, thinking what it was I really wanted. Worrying about what the right choice was. Worrying, despite Dr. Griffith's continued reassurance, that something was terribly wrong with my baby.

What *did* I really want?

Turned out, what I really wanted was Rogan. But I worried if a relationship between us didn't work out, I would lose our friendship, and that scared me more than the idea of not trying at all. Was the chance worth it?

"I think I would like…" I paused to lick my lips, which suddenly felt terribly dry. "I think I would like to try taking our relationship further," I spit it all out in a rush of words that barely sounded sensible to my own ears. "But I'm scared." I didn't look at Rogan when I said it, instead keeping my eyes focused on the scenes buzzing past the window.

The gap of time between when I spat out my hopes and when Rogan finally spoke seemed so long, I began to despair.

When he did speak, his voice had a low tremble running beneath it, a thick undercurrent of emotion. "I've wanted a relationship with you since I first met you, Keisha. That hasn't changed. But if you're sure this is what you want, if you're serious, then we need to have a talk."

"About what?" He sounded so ominous, I felt a flutter of anxiety in my stomach. I clenched the door handle to keep myself grounded.

He flicked a glance in my direction. "Life. Family. My family, in particular. And yours, unless I'm entirely mistaken."

What?

"*My* family? What family? Mim and my mother are all I've got, and my mother is barely even in my life. What do either of them have to do with us?"

"More than you probably realize, sweetheart. But we'll plan a time to talk this over. It will take a while."

Just as I had gotten some semblance of a life plan together, the man I've decided to dedicate myself to throws me for a loop. A really, really weird loop. To say I felt confused would be a vast understatement. "I'm confused." It wasn't much, but I honestly couldn't think of anything else to say. Houses, cars, and trees whipped by in a blur. Perfect metaphor for my current brain situation.

"I'm sure," he said agreeably. "There's a lot to consider."

"Rogan." I was beginning to feel as though we were having two entirely different conversations. "You aren't making any sense."

He laughed. Though, I didn't get the sense he was laughing *at* me, it still irked me.

"It will all make sense in due time, sweetheart. Just trust me. We're almost there."

We're almost there. I repeated his words in my mind. I knew he meant we were almost to Dr. Griffith's, but it meant so much more to me in that moment.

We're almost there. The words also had me rubbing my hands over the swell of my belly and I wondered what my baby would look like. T-shirts had gotten too tight to wear, and I'd finally let Layla drag me into town to buy some maternity clothes. Just a few more months, and I'd know who was in there, making my back ache and craving spicy chili.

We're almost there. After months of friendship that bordered on something more, we were really doing this, deciding together to move forward with a relationship.

I felt as though I was teetering at the edge of a high building, getting ready to jump and hoping my parachute worked.

"Tell me about your mother," Rogan said, as we sat across from one another at his dining table, a mountain of food between us.

It was the night of the *big talk*, the expected official beginning of our relationship. Rogan had surprised me by driving me back to his house, which was a single-wide trailer in a small park that was mainly inhabited by senior citizens. It was a nice place on a neat little rectangle lot. His was one of the few in the park that didn't have plastic pink flamingos out front.

Inside looked much like a cabin, with lots of wood, flannel and an electric fireplace at the far end of the living room, which Rogan turned on just before we started dinner, although it was eighty-five degrees outside. The hum of the window air conditioning unit battled against the crackling of the faux fire.

There was no television.

Setting my fork back on the plate, I considered the question. "Well, to begin with, she's white."

Barking out a laugh, Rogan pointed at me with the roll he was about to take a bite of. "That's not what I meant, and you know it."

I still wasn't certain where this conversation was going, but it seemed important to him, so I plunged ahead, "Her name is Kelly. Kelly Lawson. She's an addict. And an occasional whore." I cringed when I heard the bitterness in my own voice, but felt unable to correct my tone. So much had gone wrong in my relationship with my mother. "She chose drugs over me a long time ago, Rogan."

Thoughtful, Rogan gazed at me, compassion lining his features. "I understand that was difficult for you, Keisha. Tell me, was she always that way?"

Again, I couldn't fathom why dredging up the past could have any importance on us, here and now. I obliged anyway, thinking back to when I was small, before my mother had chosen a path that didn't include me. "When I was a little girl, she tried to make things work. After my father left, she was on her own and she struggled with that quite a lot. She used to work two, sometimes three part-time jobs, trying to keep the rent paid and food on the table. During that time, I spent a lot of time at Mim's house. When I was about eight, my mother decided to try going back to school. She signed up at the local community college, and dropped out two months later. That was just the first in a long string of failed attempts. In between those times, she would go back to working, but she was getting older, and got tired more easily. That, as far as I'm aware, is about the time she started doing drugs."

Rogan mumbled something under his breath, took a sip of water, and motioned for me to go on.

I paused, thinking back. Though the last several years of my teenage life had been rotten, I remembered when I was younger and Mom hadn't been so bad. I had flashes of times when she had braided my hair while I watched cartoons, or laid on my bedroom floor with me, coloring pictures of princesses to tape to my walls.

"She changed, then. Lost weight. Her eyes were bloodshot most of the time, and she rarely slept. I remember noticing her hands shaking often." I recalled with sudden clarity a morning I found her sprawled across the kitchen linoleum, eyes half shut, drool running from her lips and puddling on the floor in front of her. I remembered the panic in my chest as I shook her, screaming for her to wake up. Wiping a hand across my face, I forced myself back to the present. "When I was about thirteen was when the guys started showing up at our place."

I watched Rogan's face as he chewed and swallowed his food. Concern replaced the earlier compassion.

"The guys?" he asked.

"Yeah. At first, she called them her boyfriends, but after a while, I realized they were the sort of men who paid for her time, and not always with money. One of them climbed into my bed one night. By *mistake*, he said." I held up two fingers on each hand and curled them down, indicating quotation marks.

"Oh, Keisha." He breathed out a deep sigh.

I waved his pity away with a swipe of my hand. "Nothing terrible happened, but after I told Mim about it, she said it would be better for everyone if I just started staying at her place more often. A year or so after that, Mom got behind on her rent and it all went to hell. She ended up on the streets, with nothing on her mind but finding ways to get more drugs."

His hand snaked across the table to envelop mine. He squeezed hard.

I noticed his big green eyes were welling with unshed tears.

The fact that Rogan was unashamed to cry around me was one of the things I'd grown to love about him. He was a sensitive person, and he owned it.

It was hard not to compare him to Vince, who acted like a macho ass most of the time because he couldn't handle his feelings. Instead, he drowned his emotions in whiskey and vodka.

Look where that had got him.

"I'm so sorry," he said.

"It's okay. Look. I turned out all right." I smiled at him then, his emotions touching my own. Spending time with Rogan was making me softer. Sweeter.

"I'm so sorry for your mother," he continued.

If I had been forced to lay bets on the things he would say this evening, I wouldn't have guessed that sentence in a million years. "For my mother? Why? She's the one who abandoned me!" Something more than irritation fired through my insides.

"Because she's hurting, Keisha. Addiction is a hard thing to battle. And because she probably has her reasons." He sounded so genuine, so sad, when he said that, my anger began to settle. "Does your mother have purple eyes? Like Mim's?"

What did that have to do with anything? "Yes," I replied slowly. "But why?"

He changed the subject abruptly and stood. "I'm going to clear up dinner. Why don't you wait for me in the living room? I'll be just a moment."

Too startled at the twist in conversation to gather my wits and say anything, I did as he asked, moving to his couch, which faced the electric fireplace. His couch was so much more comfortable – and attractive – than the ugly plaid one in Layla's camper.

"I don't own a television, but there's a stack of books under the end table right there," he called from the kitchen. "Feel free."

I loved to read, always had. I'd taken several books with me to Windy Springs, but had already blown through all of them. Searching the space beneath the small wooden table, I found one that looked promising and plucked it out.

Rogan's "just a moment" seemed to be dragging out to a much longer length of time. I waited, trying to stay patient and worked to lose myself in the story, though I had a hard time focusing. Tonight was supposed to be special for us. Rogan had expressed repeatedly that he had something important to discuss with me. I couldn't begin to imagine what it might be, but had made extra effort with my appearance in expectation of the evening. My long, frizzy black hair was tied neatly up in a bun, with soft tendrils slipping out here and there around my face. I'd put on makeup – not the Ren faire, fairyland creature sort – but actual smoky eye, blush, and red lipstick. My nails were painted dark red as well, to match the tiny red flowers on my sundress, which was the prettiest article of maternity clothing I owned. Excepting the apparent watermelon stuffed under my dress, I thought I looked a little better than decent.

Forcing my eyes back to the page, I tried to pay attention to the story, but my brain just wasn't having it. I'd read the same first paragraph six times. The heat from the electric fireplace was making me sleepy, and I fought to keep my eyes open.

"Keisha?" Rogan shook my shoulder. "Wake up."

I pushed myself to a sitting position, my eyes darting around the room as I tried to orient myself to my surroundings. *Where was I? Oh, right. Rogan's house.* "Rogan," I mumbled, my voice thick still with sleep.

"You passed out. Tired, sweetheart? I brought you some tea." He offered me the cup. I must not have seemed overly excited, because he asked, "What? I thought you liked tea."

"I *drink* tea. Not because I like it. But because it's uncaffeinated. Thank you, though. I'll drink it," I said, staring into the cup.

Sipping on our tea, we sat there in quiet, companionable silence for several minutes.

"Sorry I fell asleep. I didn't mean to, but you took so long."

"I love it when you politely chastise me that way." He laughed. "I apologize for taking so long. I cleaned up dinner, and then I spent a little while thinking about how to say what I need to say."

"You keep saying things like that, and it makes me feel like something terrible is about to happen." Anxiety knotted up my stomach, and saliva pooled in my cheeks. I clutched my cup of tea like it could stave off whatever was coming.

The décor in the room suited Rogan, somehow, and he seemed at ease as he reclined next to me on the couch. Leaning forward, he set his empty cup on the coffee table and released a heavy sigh. "Do you trust me?" he asked, his fingers drumming against his knees.

I recognized that action for the symptom of nerves that it was, despite his relaxed appearance. It struck me with a jolt that without realizing it, I had begun picking up on Rogan's nonverbal cues.

The thought of that put a silly little smile on my face.

"I trust you," I replied, completely serious, reaching one hand out to drop over his drumming fingers, stilling them.

He took a deep breath and blew it out. "Keisha, I'm about to tell you something that will sound unbelievable. But I want you to believe me, to trust me. Will you?"

There was such a somber expression on his face, I felt compelled to say the right thing, though I couldn't fathom what his news was about. "I don't think you would lie to me, Rogan." This was true. I didn't think he would deliberately tell me a lie.

He laughed, though the sound was mirthless. "That's not what I asked you, Keisha. I'm asking, if I tell you something so wild it's completely unbelievable, will you still trust I am speaking the truth?"

Blind trust was a hard thing for me to practice. My previous relationships – with my mother, with Vince – had built a wall inside me, making it a struggle to believe someone just on their word alone.

But this was Rogan. Rogan was different, he had proved this to me over and over.

I made a choice.

"I'll believe you, Rogan," I said.

CHAPTER TWELVE

He'd been waiting for me to say something. I knew that.

But there were no words I could find that would encompass my current thoughts.

There was a special ability that ran in his family, he said. 'Knowing', it was called.

And Rogan thought it ran in my family, too.

Knowing, he told me, was the ability to see things that other people couldn't.

The occasional talent for communicating with those who were dead, or someone who was far away but gravely ill.

There was a spectrum of Knowing, Rogan explained. For some, like him, it was an occasional feeling, or sight. He could sense danger sometimes. He had visions of things to come. He could, with the help of others like him, change the thoughts of a weak-minded person, though he promised me such an action wasn't a thing he took lightly.

Those further down the spectrum had stronger abilities, more intense and frequent communications with the dead or those who were deathly ill. They often heard the voices of those pleading for help, even of those they didn't know personally, echoing over and over in their minds.

These were the ones who were born with purple eyes.

These were the ones, Rogan said, who often ended up as addicts, taking drug after drug or drinking themselves into a stupor on a daily basis, all in an effort to numb the voices, the pleas, in their minds.

Despite my resolve to believe him, no matter what he said, my initial inclination was to get up and leave his house.

He was obviously screwing with me. With my trust. My mind.

Why would he do this? After how far we'd come, all the things we had talked about, the times we were brutally honest with one another.

Why would he lie to me now?

I couldn't comprehend it, though his words spun round and round in my mind. "I don't understand this, Rogan."

How could I? How could I understand such a notion? How could I accept it?

Two things kept me frozen in place on the couch, as I watched the fake flames flickering in the electric fireplace.

One was that, regardless of what he was telling me now, I didn't want to lose him, and I knew if I walked out of his home, that's exactly what would happen. Our budding relationship would be out the window, and there would be no more happy conversations over chili bread bowls during our lunch breaks at the festival, no more evenings laughing as we sat in the chairs outside Layla's camper. No more discussions about books, or the baby, or our future together.

It was then I realized how much I loved him.

I'd known I cared for him. Had known it for weeks now. Cared enough to want to pursue a serious relationship with him. To consider having him in my child's life.

But in that moment, I recognized my feelings for what they were: love. It was real and intense.

I was in love with Rogan, and I didn't want to lose what we had.

The other thing was what Rogan said about people with Knowing having purple eyes.

My mother. Mim.

Purple eyes.

Images flashed through my mind of my mother, her frantic pace throughout life, her struggle with drugs and alcohol. The many, many men that had come and gone over the years.

What if—what if it all had been a fight to numb her mind to the things she saw, the things she heard?

What if it wasn't her fault?

The baby tumbled inside me, and I placed a hand over my swollen belly, thinking.

My own eyes were brown.

Mim's words replayed in my head, what she'd said the day I had told her I was pregnant.

I'll always know. And the curse goes on.

I'd put it down to the ramblings of a confused old woman, but what if…?

And that was the question, really.

What if?

What if the Knowing was real?

"I don't understand it, but I will choose to believe you," I said finally.

As I wrestled with the idea of Knowing, of Rogan, and possibly my mother and grandmother having this ability, I remembered something else.

The day Vince had come after me at Windy Springs, when I had first met Captain Dash, he'd asked a question of our table at large.

"She's knowing, isn't she?" he'd asked casually.

"Actually, my name is Keisha," I'd responded, like an idiot. I had assumed he had been hitting the mead too hard. But maybe he was—was one of them. Or at least, he knew about them.

Was I surrounded by these Knowing people?

Rogan had been silent, allowing me time to digest this information.

"Is Captain Dash Knowing?" I blurted.

"Yes."

I expected him to elaborate on that, but he didn't. He just sat there, watching me, waiting for me to come to grips with it all.

"Is Jack? Is Layla?" Oh, my God. I could suddenly see the possibility that everyone else in the world was one of them, except me.

"Jack, yes. Layla, no. But Layla is aware of it. Nearly everyone at the festival is aware of Knowing, even if they don't necessarily understand what it's all about."

"Why are there so many of them, of the Knowing people, there?" Once, when I had expressed concern that I wouldn't fit in at the Ren faire, Layla had laughed and told me everyone fit in there. It was one place where everyone would be welcomed.

And it was true. Everyone fit in there. Cosplayers. Introverts. Extroverts. Artists. Actors. Geeks. I'd noticed the welcoming nature of the "Rennies" shortly after I'd begun working at On a Wing and a Prayer.

I had looked at the melding of different personalities, at the inclusion of people who often lived on the fringes of society, and thought Layla had been right. The reality was, I had very little idea how inclusive Windy Springs truly was. Apparently, even the owner of the festival had this strange mind ability, and others like him were flocking there.

"We can sense one another. And it turns out that many of us happen to be creative types." He shrugged. "Ren faire is a great cover. And it's fun."

I'd spent months among these people, thinking them slightly strange for preferring to dress like pirates, fairies and a myriad of other fairytale creatures or cosplay figures, but finding in the end, they were goodhearted, unique people just looking for an outlet for their creativity.

Now I knew something else united them. Well, most of them. A bizarre ability drawing them together, an entire other reality from the one I'd known all my life, and everyone around me, everyone who was supposed to love me, had kept me from knowing the truth.

"I feel lied to." If we were going to do the truth thing, I was all in. My voice was heavy, thick with emotion, with sudden understanding.

With hurt.

Because it hurt me that none of them had told me. Not my own mother, or even Mim. What if I had turned out to be Knowing, and they hadn't prepared me for it? Wasn't that a mother's job, to prepare her child for their life? Especially, if it was possible I had some weird ability?

It was just one more area my mother had failed me in.

And Mim, well, she'd always been on the strong side of strange, but surely she could have put forth the effort where my mother had not, to tell me of my roots, of my heritage.

Of this thing, this massive, bizarre trait I could one day pass on to my own children.

My baby. My *baby*.

Oh, no.

I felt as though the floor was caving in, about to swallow us up, couch and all. "Rogan," I whispered. "How will I know if my baby has it? Knowing?"

His green eyes were wide and honest, and as soon as he began to speak, I knew in my heart he was already aware of what my baby was or was not. Somehow… Somehow, he knew.

"A hallmark of carrying a child with Knowing is that the mother often feels – despite normal test results – that something is wrong. You've told me yourself that's something you've felt since the beginning." He stopped, and I knew he was carefully considering his next words.

"Will it—harm my baby at all? Does it hurt?" The thought that I had unwittingly passed a trait I wasn't aware I had carried on to my baby, a trait that could cause pain to him or her, was making me feel ill. And dizzy. I leaned my head back against the couch cushion.

"Physically, it doesn't cause pain of any kind, other than sometimes headaches when the voices get to be too much. Mentally—" He stopped, seeming to gather his courage to tell me something unpleasant, "Mentally, it can be a challenge, and is why so many fall victim to addiction. Without someone to guide these children, to teach them how to manage it, having the ability can cause a person to become self-destructive." He waited, watching me to see how I would accept the knowledge.

I remembered the visceral tug I'd felt toward Rogan back in May. Could my baby have sensed it? Drawn me to him? The thought of it was disturbing. "Your parents, Rogan? Were they…?" I asked. He'd told me his family was all gone, and I hadn't pushed to find out more, expecting he would tell me when he felt the time was right. But this was one thing I needed to know.

"Yes, they were." He sighed, rubbed his forehead. His eyes looked suddenly weary, the slight lines around them deepening. "They both were Knowing, and I loved my parents, but neither of them could handle their ability. I spent a lot of time in and out of foster care, because they were not always able to care for me properly. I didn't have a Mim," he added, wistful. "It was just the three of us. And two of the three had a problem with heroin."

"Oh, Rogan," I said, wishing I could erase some of what he had probably lived through as a child. I could relate to that sort of misery. It hurt me to think Rogan had suffered the same way. At least, I'd had Mim. Who had Rogan had to guide him, help him with homework, tuck him in at night?

My heart ached for the boy he'd been, knocked around to different foster homes, all the while learning to manage his ability on his own. "It's surprising you didn't go that way. Drugs, I mean."

"No," he said vehemently, "I wouldn't do that. I watched what it did to my parents, and ultimately, bad heroin is what took them completely from me. Knowing can be a hardship, but it has plenty of good points, too. I've helped people Keisha. People, who needed me, people who were desperate and called out to me. I focus on that part of it, not the other. If all I did was think about how it's ruined my life, I'd lose my mind."

Through the half-open blinds in his living room, I could see the light was waning. The hum of the central air unit was the only sound between us.

Rogan slipped his arm around my shoulders and pulled me to him. "I know it's a lot to process. Take your time."

Mentally, I railed against it. It would be easy enough to blow his story of Knowing off as a prank or even a mental disorder. The thing was, it made so much sense. It explained so many things. And the more he told me, the more I understood it, as though the knowledge had always been there inside of me, like puzzle pieces just waiting to be dropped into place.

As the truth settled over me, my skin erupted in gooseflesh and I shivered.

Rogan tightened his hold on me, as though by doing so he could squeeze his own strength into my quivering bones. "Now that you understand, Keisha, maybe you can see why I wanted to have this talk with you before we decided to jump into a relationship. Before, you told me you were ready. Now that you know, are you ready still? Do you still want this with me?"

Yes, I decided. I did. I still wanted him, wanted his strong arms around me, wanted his laughter, his smile and his beautiful green eyes to look into mine for the rest of my life.

Rogan may not have been what others saw as 'traditionally handsome,' whatever that meant. When I had first met him, I'd been guilty of dismissing him because of his height and his looks, though so much of that had been a costume. But as I'd come to know him over this summer, I had come to see a man who was kind and funny, generous and steady.

I wanted to tell him the way I felt. I wanted to tell him I was in love with him, that I never wanted anyone else but him.

But the words failed me. It'd been so long since I had said those words to anyone, and though it was clear in my mind what I wanted to say, the words lodged in my throat, stubbornly refusing to come out.

Rogan was waiting. His grip on me hadn't wavered in the least. His breaths were strong and steady as I kept my head against his chest.

What was going through his mind?

How could I explain what I was feeling? This intense, almost painful, emotion that filled me through my bones, my soul?

I couldn't. But I could show him.

Clumsily at first, given the girth of my middle, I rose up on my knees, steadying myself with my hands on his shoulders. He released his hold on me, his hands moving to rest on my hips. Staring into his eyes, I cradled his face in my hands. When my lips met his, he opened his mouth to me and a soft, sighing sound escaped him.

Our first kiss.

It deepened, and all the pent up longing I'd been holding in for weeks on end burst forth. My hands seemed to be moving of their own volition, stroking Rogan's head, face, arms, and chest. Heat sparked through my core, leaving me breathless with anticipation.

It'd been so long since I felt this way. Desire had been gone from my relationship with Vince long before I had made the choice to leave. Then I had been too distraught and too nauseated to consider a romantic relationship. For months, I had thought of Rogan as a friend and nothing more.

But now… now it was different.

Finally, the words that had been trapped in my throat burst forth, and I pressed my cheek against Rogan's when I told him the one thing I had been waiting to say. "I love you," I breathed, feeling stronger for having said it.

Rogan shuddered, as though a shock had jolted through his entire body, and this time, I was the one holding *him* tight.

Emboldened, I went on, "I want you, Rogan." My senses were entirely focused on him, on us, on how it would feel for us to join together that way, skin on skin.

"Keisha," he mumbled, filling his fists with my hair, tugging. His breath coming in short, haggard spurts.

Desire for Rogan had amped up to the point where I didn't think I could bear to wait any longer and I felt feral, clawing at his clothes, no longer a thought in my head that didn't include getting his clothes off, and figuring out which door led to the bedroom.

Not that I *needed* a bedroom for this, but given my current shape and size, I figured it would be slightly less awkward on a bed than attempting a tumble on the couch.

I'd managed to get his shirt unbuttoned and shoved off one shoulder. It was the first time I'd seen this part of him and the thrill that shot through me at the sight of his bare skin acted as fuel to urge me on in my mission. No longer shivering, sweat broke out down my spine and across my forehead. I could feel strands of my hair sticking to my face.

"Keisha," he said again, this time with more force.

"Yes," I replied, nearly breathless with need. "Yes, Rogan."

He grabbed my wrists, shoving me back against the couch. It took me a second to situate my legs, dragging them out from beneath me. Rogan pushed harder, pinning my arms above my head, and a giddy rush of adrenaline zipped through my senses. Writhing against him, I whimpered, begging him not to make me wait any more. "Please, Rogan. *Please.*" My eyes were shut, and I could feel his breath, heavy on my skin.

"Sweetheart."

His voice sounded thick, drenched in emotion, and I readied myself for the moment I'd been waiting for.

"Wait."

My eyes snapped open, my breaths at this point coming in uneven gasps. My chest was literally heaving. Less in the way of a Hollywood starlet, and more in the way of an asthmatic on a frantic search for their inhaler.

That's how I felt, to be honest. Like I needed air and having Rogan inside me would be the only way to get it.

Rogan was my inhaler. Romance at its finest.

"What?" I stared up at him, working to make sense of his words. I shook my head to clear it, in case I'd somehow heard him wrong. "What?" I asked again. I gulped air, starving for it.

Starving for Rogan.

"I said, wait. Slow down a minute, Keisha."

I couldn't read the expression on his face. Frustrated, maybe. But I was freely offering him a venue to release his frustration. It didn't make any sense.

Moving off me, he slumped back, dragging the back of his hand across his face.

I pressed my palm against my chest, as though that would somehow slow the frenetic beating of my heart. I was still half-lying on the couch, my legs stuck out at odd angles, my belly making a mountain between us.

After a few minutes of silence, he helped me up to a sitting position. I felt mildly less vulnerable that way, but my level of confusion had gone through the roof. My breathing was beginning to level off to something near normal. "I don't understand, Rogan." Since my brain was slowing down and I could formulate thoughts that included something beyond tearing off Rogan's clothes, the feeling of rejection hit me with physical force. "You—you don't want me?" I could hear the hitch in my voice.

If he'd had hair, he would have been running his hands through it. Instead, he just kept rubbing his bald head. He pursed his lips, blowing out a long breath. "That's not the case at all, Keisha. I *do* want you. And I love you, so much sometimes, it hurts me." Furrowing his brows, he seemed to be reaching for the right words, so I stayed quiet.

Waiting. I was always waiting, it seemed.

I felt so sick of it. I didn't want to wait anymore.

But the man I'd fallen in love with was demanding I do just that.

"Listen, sweetheart," he said, his eyes resting not on me, but on the ceiling. "I need to explain something to you."

Great. Another explanation. What was he going to say next, he could turn invisible? He could fly?

Reverting to my former champion nodding skills, I bobbed my head up and down. Might as well get it all out in the open, whatever it was.

"I told you before, my last relationship ended badly."

Up and down, up and down, my head went. It was a wonder I hadn't shaken my brain into oblivion.

"I've been waiting for five years. Five *years,* Keisha. Because I think it's worth it to wait. To wait for what's right, because I want my next relationship to last forever." Leaning forward, he put his elbows on his knees. When he spoke again, his voice was heavier. Deeper. Laden with the feelings he was trying to express, "And I was right, because you, Keisha, you were worth the wait." He laced his fingers with mine, squeezing hard as he cleared his throat. "You haven't been treated the way you should have been, sweetheart. Not by Vince, not by your mother. You are so precious to me. I want you to know your worth."

The baby kicked, creating a visible movement beneath my flowered dress, and Rogan put his free hand on my belly, feeling that promise of life. Of a future. Of family.

Family.

Something we'd both been lacking in our lives.

"I'll be honest here, Rogan. I'm not feeling much worth right this minute. I'm feeling pretty rejected."

Immediately, he pressed my hand to his lips. "No, sweetheart. Oh, no. I don't want you to ever feel rejection from me."

"But you—?"

"Sssh." He cut me off, slipping from the couch and landing on his knees. Still with his fingers laced through mine, he removed his other hand from my belly to jam it into his pocket.

I blew some errant wisps of hair up and out of my face. I imagined my makeup was smeared. The top of my dress looked askew, and I adjusted it as I waited for him to go on with his explanation. When I looked up from fixing the neck of my dress,

Rogan was holding a thick, silver ring between his thumb and forefinger.

A deep pink tinge spread across his cheeks, and his big green eyes welled up with unshed tears.

I was having that problem again, where the words shooting around in my brain were blocked from emerging audibly. I opened my mouth and shut it, unable to get any sound out.

I imagined I resembled a hungry baby bird.

Affecting a terrible, faux British accent, Rogan spoke slowly, his voice caressing each word as though it was treasure. "M'lady," he began, "it would pleasure me deeply if you would consent to be my bride. Would you consider accepting this ring?" He held it toward me, and though he was smiling, the hand holding the ring trembled visibly.

My first inclination was to scream yes. Though I felt startled Rogan would propose after us knowing each other such a short time, there was no doubt in my mind this was what I wanted. I wanted a future, a forever, with the man kneeling before me.

In my heart, my soul, I wanted this.

Again, my mouth opened and shut, but my vocal chords still seemed temporarily frozen.

Rogan was waiting for my answer.

In the absence of a voice, I did the one thing I could still do like a champ.

I nodded.

The tears that had been welling in Rogan's eyes finally fell.

CHAPTER THIRTEEN

"I cannot marry you next week, Rogan!" He was being ridiculous. I pushed against the mattress, awkwardly shifting my body into a sitting position, resting my head on the wooden headboard and my hands on my belly.

I had spent the night at his place. Our first time sleeping together had been just that – sleeping.

I would be worth the wait, he kept telling me.

As long, apparently, as that wait only lasted another week.

"In two weeks, then." He grinned up at me from where he lay, his head surrounded by the pattern of green vines on his pillow.

"We need time to get a venue. I need a dress. And flowers and things. I don't even know how long it takes to get a marriage license."

Propping himself up on one elbow, he traced my jaw with a finger. Then my throat.

Slowly, he dragged his finger down lower, and gooseflesh rippled over my skin. A loud gasp escaped me, and I gripped the sheets, twisting them up in my fist. "Rogan," I breathed.

"What if I said we already have a venue?" The expression on his face told me he had something up his sleeve. Or he would have, if he'd had on a shirt, which he didn't.

His lack of sleeves was pretty to look at, and I ran my tongue across my lips. "You're being ridiculous," I repeated. "Besides, you're deliberately distracting me."

"I am? How?"

He knew exactly how.

"You know, in the far back of Windy Springs, there's that wooden arch with the flowers all over it?"

I'd seen it, though it was far from On a Wing and a Prayer and I didn't often go that way. I had heard they sometimes did handfasting ceremonies there, but since I didn't exactly understand what a handfasting was, I hadn't paid it all that much attention.

"Windy Springs keeps a nondenominational minister contracted per diem. He asks for a forty-eight-hour notice for handfasting or marriage ceremonies. Two weeks gives us plenty of time." He wiggled his eyebrows up and down. "I can call him today."

He wasn't understanding. We couldn't just get married that fast. "I can't marry you in two weeks, either, Rogan."

"Why? You said you loved me."

"I *do* love you."

"Then why wait?"

He clearly thought it all made sense in his own mind.

"For one thing, I'm pregnant." I patted my rounded belly to remind him.

"It's not like I hadn't noticed that," he stated wryly.

"Well, I..." I sputtered. "I'll look like I'm wearing a tent, instead of a wedding gown. I want to look pretty."

He sat up, brushing tenderly at my wild case of bed head, and kissed me deeply, passionately. Then pulling away, he spoke, "Keisha..." His eyes were lit with desire, "you are without a doubt the most beautiful woman I have ever met. Even if all you wore to our wedding was a tent, I would still find you absolutely stunning." He seemed so sincere, so earnest, I almost believed him.

"It's not just that," I whispered. I wished I was the kind of person – like Layla – who didn't care what other people thought of me, but I wasn't.

"Tell me sweetheart. Tell me what's really bothering you about this."

I diverted my eyes from his, fixing my gaze instead on the pattern of the comforter. "I'm embarrassed that everyone knows you aren't the father of my baby. Everyone *knows.* They'll—

they'll think I'm a…" I wasn't even sure what I thought everyone would think of me, but I knew it wouldn't be nice.

I remembered the way people had looked at my mother when they realized what she did for money.

When they saw man after man leaving our home, all hours of the day and night.

I didn't think I could handle it if the people I'd come to consider my friends looked at me that way.

"They'll think you are Keisha, their friend that they have come to know and care for over the last several months. They'll see you are happy and in love and they will be glad you found someone to share your life with. Rennies stick together, Keisha. They consider you one of us. Friendship and support is the foundation of the festival."

"You're sure?" I still couldn't manage to get my voice above a whisper.

"I'm sure," Rogan replied, as he dropped kisses all over my forehead.

I took a deep breath and let it out. "Rogan?"

He paused his apparent pursuit of kissing the entirety of my face to answer me, "Yes, sweetheart?"

I reached up to cradle his head against my neck, relishing the way his stubble-lined head felt on my skin.

I wanted to feel this every morning of my life.

"Call the guy."

For once in all the years I had known Layla, she was speechless.

I'd expected her to jump up and down and do that squealing thing she usually did when she was excited, but instead she sat there at the table that folded down into her bed at night, chin propped in her hands, staring at me.

It had been ten minutes since I told her Rogan and I were getting married. I'd been watching the clock on the miniature microwave. "You're going to have to get on board with this, Lay. I want you to be my maid of honor."

Silence.

"Talk, Layla. Are you happy? Sad? Mad? I need to know." Biting my bottom lip, I wondered what I would do if she refused to come to the wedding.

The wedding that was in two weeks. *Two weeks.* Oh, my God. What had I agreed to do?

Finally, she spoke, her voice a flat monotone, "There's no way I can do it."'

My heart softened toward her. It'd probably come as a pretty big shock. I was still trying to process it. "Oh, Lay, of course you can. I think Rogan's going to ask Jack to stand up with him, so maybe you can walk together. It's going to be low key, nothing fancy."

She shook her head, eyes still stunned. "Even if I start now and work until the wedding, I'll never be done in time."

Every time I thought I had a grip on a conversation lately, it took some bizarre twist.

"Done with what?" I asked. I could feel the confusion on my face.

"Your wedding dress!" she nearly shouted. "You can't just throw this on me with only two weeks to work!"

I was beginning to catch on. I hoped.

"You don't need to make me anything, Lay. I can just buy something at one of the shops in town. Come with me and we'll both get dresses. Make it a girls' day. It will be fun!" I said brightly.

I was trying to stay positive.

Layla wasn't aware that Rogan had told me about Knowing. I'd planned to tell her, but given her reaction to the news of the wedding, maybe I would wait until she was a little calmer.

"Of course, I'm going to make your wedding dress! There isn't a question about it. I could do something simple, maybe. Mundane, or Ren?"

Mundanes, or 'Danes' for short, I had learned over the summer, was what Rennies called outsiders.

"I'm not certain," I replied. Before this summer, I had entertained the occasional daydream of myself on my wedding day, wearing one of those dresses that made the bride look like she was a cupcake about to be gobbled up. But considering how much my life had changed over the last several months, maybe I would buck the norm and do something completely different. "Ren, I think. Can we do that?"

Layla was lost to me, already tucked away in her own mind, scribbling on a napkin a picture of what looked like a fairy bride, complete with wings.

"I'm not wearing wings to get married in, Lay," I said, peering over her shoulder at her design.

"Hush," she replied, waving a dismissive hand in my direction. "I know what I'm doing. Trust me."

There would be no deterring her.

That's the thing about Layla. She's stubborn as the day is long.

Sighing, I gave up, at least for the moment. "Try to make me something that doesn't emphasize the enormous belly, okay?" She could do that much for me.

"Sshh," she hissed. "I'm working."

It was only my wedding, after all. Why should I have any say in it?

September 2010

It was ten weeks until my due date, and three days until my wedding.

Layla had been cleaning, I thought, as I let the thin metal door of the camper fall shut behind me. I'd been reading outside in one of the fold-up camping chairs, when Layla shouted for me. Setting my book down on the tiny counter, I took in the heavy scent of baby wipes.

She must have gone through an entire box of them.

Might as well get used to the smell of them, I thought, as I rubbed my belly.

"What's up, Lay?" I asked, peeking around the miniature refrigerator.

Layla looked high. Green eyes blazing, cheeks flushed, red curls sprouting haphazardly from her head. "Time for your fitting!" she said in a loud, singsong voice.

Since the day we had picked out the material for my dress, Layla had spent every spare moment hunched over her sewing machine. Now, she stood triumphantly in front of the orange plaid couch, holding my wedding dress by the shoulders, beaming.

My hand flitted to my chest, resting flat above my heart. "Oh, Layla," I breathed. "It's beautiful." I moved forward to touch it.

Layla slapped my arm. "Wash your hands first," she demanded. "I can't just throw this in a washing machine if you get it dirty, you know."

I obediently scrubbed up at the kitchen sink, washing all the way up to my elbows.

Slipping off my sundress – I almost always wore sundresses now, except during festival hours, as they were the only comfortable thing to wear – I soaked up the sensations as Layla dropped my wedding gown over me.

"Don't move much," she cautioned. "There are still pins in some places."

The fabric looked gauzy, with a hint of sparkle to it, and was dark green.

After some discussion, we had decided against white, for obvious reasons.

The sleeves were long and flowy, while the high waist left the fabric falling softly over my rounded belly. The rolled hem stopped just past my ankles.

If I had been a weepy sort of woman, I would have cried then. "It's perfect, Lay. Thank you."

She patted my shoulder. "I know it is, but we aren't done just yet. I have a little surprise for you." Carefully lifting the lid of a small box that had been sitting on the table, Layla removed something shiny and round.

Using both hands, she presented me with a crown.

About two inches deep, it was fashioned from long, thin sticks woven together. Jewels and small pebbles of all different colors had been set in various places, and as she tipped it into the light, the jewels picked up the sun, making them sparkle.

"I love you, Layla," I said, engulfing her in a hug, being careful not to get myself stabbed by any pins still in the dress. "Thank you."

"You're going to squash your crown! Let me go."

"Never," I said, squeezing her harder.

"I don't understand why I can't see the dress," Rogan whined as he helped load the wagon to take another several boxes of wings back to On a Wing and a Prayer.

I dug my fist into my lower back as we entered the forest. The bigger I got, the more my back hurt. I hated to think how it would feel by November. "You can wait until tomorrow, Rogan. Be patient. Besides, you're the one who is such a champion of waiting for everything," I teased.

He groaned dramatically, pulling the wagon over a big lump in the path.

"It's only fair. I don't have any idea what you'll be wearing tomorrow, either."

"I could show you," he replied, hopeful. "I'll model it for you tonight, after closing."

"Nope. I want to be surprised." I pulled a pair of wings from the box to put out.

"Have I told you lately, how mean you are?"

"No, but Layla has, so no worries," I deadpanned. "It's only twenty-six hours until the wedding, Rogan. You can do this."

"Not happily," he responded, lugging another box from the wagon.

Laughter rang out as Layla and Jack strode down the lane toward us. She'd been slacking on helping with the set-up of On a Wing and a Prayer this morning, but she deserved the break after working so hard on my dress. Her hands had been so sore last night from hand-sewing tiny green beads to the bodice of my dress that I had spent half an hour massaging them for her.

"What's up, Gibble?" Layla asked, still laughing from whatever it was Jack had said that got her giggling in the first place. She wiped her eyes and took a deep breath, evidently attempting to calm herself down.

"Rogan," I corrected.

Layla rolled her eyes. "Right. Rogan. Sorry."

"She won't let me see the dress," he complained, jerking his thumb in my direction.

Having none of it, Layla replied, "Good for her. You just have to wait. Nobody gets to see it until tomorrow."

"Dad!" Jack said, and a deep, booming voice greeted him.

It could only be one person.

Captain Dash.

I spun slowly, unsure why he was here at On a Wing and a Prayer. He'd never stopped by previously, and I had the feeling he'd come for something serious. He *looked* serious.

As serious as a chronic pirate with golden dreadlocks and a mildly loose grasp on sanity could look, of course.

Puffy white shirt. Loose black pants stuffed into his boot tops. Various natures of weapons lined his belts. The dark leather tricorn perched atop his long dreadlocks was what really pulled the look all together.

"Keisha," he said, holding his arms out as he walked toward me.

Instinct made me want to back up, but I stayed rooted to my spot.

He threw his arms around me, holding me tight.

His dreads tickled my face. I struggled to get a deep breath. Alarmed, I met Rogan's eyes, wishing I knew the proper amount of Morse code blinks to signal for help.

His face looked red and he had one hand clamped over his mouth. His eyes were watering, though rather than evidence of his typical sensitive nature, this was clearly caused by his attempt to keep from guffawing.

Captain Dash held me tight in his embrace, rubbing circles on my back with a hand that felt so large, it seemed to encompass the width of my back.

And my fiancé just stood there, watching as his boss nearly squeezed the life out of me.

Finally, Dash pulled back, his eyes soft, pupils dilated. "A wedding in the woods is afoot, I'm told."

"It is, Captain Dash. Tomorrow, after closing."

His hand slid from my back around to my belly, where it sat for several seconds.

I didn't move. I barely breathed. Layla, Jack, and Rogan seemed frozen as well.

"The child is Knowing," He stated the words with such finality. Such authority.

This time, I knew what he meant. "Yes," I replied. I was sure of it. I had so much more to learn about the ability before my baby was born. The feeling that something was wrong with my child still clung to me like a sticky layer of dirt. Still caused me nightmares. But at least now I knew why.

I had so many questions for Rogan, but they would have to wait.

Captain Dash heaved a deep sigh. "I'll do it, then," he said, "I own the festival, after all. It's my place. I'm the captain of the ship."

I hoped someone else would step into this bizarre, nonsensical conversation and help me out, but all three of them remained silent, standing a few feet away from me and the crazy Captain.

"I'm sorry, Captain Dash. I'm confused. You'll do what, exactly?" The thought flitted through my mind that there was some sort of ritual expected after the baby's birth and he was offering to do it, whatever *it* was.

The look on his face indicated he thought I might be a little slow. "Walk you down the aisle. Give you away, to your man, here."

"Oh… that's kind of you to offer. I was planning to walk down the aisle by myself."

His hand remained on my belly. The baby kicked, and a slow smile spread across his face.

He shook his head, golden dreadlocks swaying back and forth. "That wouldn't be appropriate. I own the festival. It's my job to do this. What time is the ceremony set to begin?"

"Seven-thirty. But—?"

Captain Dash clicked his heels together, saluting me before taking a step back and bowing. "Tomorrow then, m'lady."

"I was going to walk by myself," I repeated as Captain Dash walked away.

"I'm not sure you're going to get a choice, Keisha," Jack explained. "Dad thinks he is responsible for everyone and everything in this forest. He takes that very seriously."

Something small scurried across my foot, and I shrieked. "I swear to God, this forest is full of rats!" I yelled, yanking my foot up, and looking around for the offending rodent.

Rogan rubbed his forehead.

Jack and Layla busied themselves setting out merchandise.

"Calm down, sweetheart, that was not a rat."

"What was it then? I keep feeling them run past me but I never see them!" Shivers crawled up my spine. I hated those little things, whatever they were.

"Remember that long talk we had at my place, right before I put this ring on your finger?"

The talk about Knowing, he meant. It was kind of hard to forget.

"Yeah. I remember. But what does that have to do with forest rodents?" I couldn't see any connection.

"There are… other things, besides Knowing, that you still need to learn about."

"Other things," I repeated. I wasn't sure I wanted to know. I was still trying to get a handle on what I'd recently learned.

The bells chimed, signaling the gates had opened.

"Later," Rogan promised. "Maybe after the wedding. For now, just remember, they aren't dangerous."

Great. So that meant what? They probably wouldn't bite me? How reassuring.

CHAPTER FOURTEEN

My wedding day.

It didn't feel as though the day was different than any of the festival days that had gone before.

Layla and I had still gotten up early to set up On a Wing and a Prayer, then Rogan and I had still eaten in the food court together during our lunch break. I had still happily plowed through a chili bread bowl while Rogan politely ate his chicken.

I was still sweating through my fairy costume while well-intentioned patrons asked about my due date and potential baby names while they sorted through various styles of wings.

In three hours, I would be cleaning up back at the camper, and Layla was going to do something with my hair before I put on my beautiful green dress.

In four hours, I would marry Rogan.

I hadn't invited Mim to the wedding. Her mind was fragile enough; I couldn't imagine watching me dressed as a fairy marrying Rogan in the woods would cause anything less than more confusion for her.

Queen Natasha and her entourage stalked past us, and Layla obediently bowed.

I couldn't muster the gumption to follow suit. I was too big. Too sweaty. And Natasha was a snot. I dipped my head and rolled my eyes until they passed, and turned back to the patron I'd been working with. "G'day, lash," I said, smiling at the young woman who'd just purchased a pair of wings. I wrapped them carefully and handed them over to her, along with her change.

"I've got a question for you, Keisha," Layla said, as the woman walked away.

"Yeah?" I asked, stuffing cash into the small leather pouch I wore dangling from the waistband of my skirt.

"I've noticed you calling women 'lash' when you're working. Why is that?"

I froze, feeling as though I'd done something wrong. "Everyone else says it. Is it wrong?" I suddenly worried it might be an insult of some kind, and I'd inadvertently been calling patrons something terrible in another language.

The side of her mouth pulled up in a smirk. "Everyone else? Who?"

Positive I was in the right, I opened my mouth to give her a list of names. But the only name that came to mind was Rogan's. "Rogan does," I defended with my chin up in defiance.

"*Rogan* does? Or Gibble?" She seemed to be enjoying her little game way too much.

"Seriously, Layla." Nobody was around. We could call him by his name.

"*Seriously, Keisha*," she mocked. "Think about it. Have you ever heard Rogan say that?"

"Well, I…"

"I can tell you right now, you haven't. Because Rogan doesn't have a lisp… only Gibble does. Because of the teeth."

Oh, my God.

She was right. I suddenly thought of all the times I'd giggled at the way his words came out, turning the "s" sound into an "sh."

"So it's not 'lash'," I said slowly. "It's…"

"Lass," we both said at the same time.

"Why did you let me keep saying it wrong the entire summer?" I demanded.

"I thought you would pick up on it!" she replied.

"You made me look stupid, Lay!" Some best friend. Good God. "Thanks a lot."

"*I* didn't do anything," she retorted smugly.

I folded my arms across my chest… which kind of hurt, because my boobs were getting tender. "If I wasn't counting on you to help me get ready for the wedding tonight, I'd be really angry."

"Well, then, good thing for me, you're getting married tonight, I guess."

That was the thing about Layla. Sometimes she was kind of a jerk.

My dress had a row of buttons running the length of my back, and I stood still in the camper as Layla did up each one. When she finished, she slipped a beautiful, intricate pair of bronze fairy wings onto me.

"You're sure the wings aren't too much?" I asked.

She shook her head. "Nah. They sort of balance out your front, if you know what I mean."

I snorted. "Gee, thanks."

"Fifteen minutes until showtime," she announced, turning me around to face her so she could fiddle with my hair.

I would have thought I would feel nervous, but I didn't. I felt happy. Settled. Peaceful.

But not nervous.

"How do I look?" I asked. My long black hair hung down, frizzy as ever, especially after a day spent working in the early September heat. Layla had parted it on the side, so one thick portion swooped across my forehead and tucked behind my ear.

She picked up my crown, and I ducked my head, so she could put it on me. I felt the weight of it on my head, and something about the moment felt reverent, almost sacred.

"You're perfect, Keisha." She wiped a tear from her eye. "You're sure this is what you want? To marry Gib – I mean, Rogan?"

"I'm sure," I said, grinning. "I know it's been fast, but I'm positive this is what I'm meant to do."

"He's a good guy, he just doesn't seem… I don't know. Like your usual type, I guess."

"My usual type? You mean alcoholic and abusive?" I raised my brows at her. I knew exactly what she was getting at. "You're right. He's not like that at all."

Throwing up her hands, she mumbled, "Fine, fine."

"Rogan is exactly who I want. There's nothing about him I would change."

Pasting on a bright smile, she placed the bouquet of wildflowers she had made for me into my hands. "All right, then. Let's go get you married, Keisha."

I stood between the rows of seats, staring at what awaited me at the end of the aisle.

Small pebbles and twigs pressed into my bare feet. I had decided to forego shoes – since all I had brought with me were my flip flops, and the brown boots Layla had given me.

Twenty feet ahead of me, Rogan stood straight, utterly dashing in his wedding clothes. Loose gray pants beneath a gray and burgundy tunic bearing a coat of arms. Long gray sleeves. And a burgundy cape that rose and fell with the slight breeze.

My knight.

Captain Dash linked his arm in mine, patting my hand as we took a step, paused, and repeated the slow wedding walk all the way down the aisle. On either side of us were fairytale creatures, pirates, belly dancers, and a myriad of other friends in garb. Juniper, the little round soap lady. Ever and Justice, the fire dancers. Grok and Bork, the Hot Gnome Brothers.

Butterflies danced in the air surrounding the flowered arch.

When we reached the front, the minister asked, "Who gives this woman to be married?"

And Dash, pulling himself up to full height, released his hold on my arm to step forward. "It is I, Captain Dashiel, owner of these woods and the festival, who gives this woman, Keisha, to be married, sire." After performing a dramatic bow, he took his seat in the left front row.

Another three steps, and I was standing next to Rogan. Turning, I handed my bouquet to Layla.

Layla, of course, was dressed like a slutty pirate. Short metallic gold tutu, striped knee socks, and a blazing red corset with no shirt underneath. Her boobs were pushed up so high she could have rested her chin on them. The breeze teased her curly red hair as she took the bouquet from me.

Dread Pirate Jack stood next to Rogan. He was dressed like… well, like Dread Pirate Jack. His beard braids had gotten longer over the summer, now nearly reaching his chest. Black hair hung over his shoulders, and his puffy white shirt gave the appearance of a girth he didn't really possess. He clutched the handle of the sword dangling from his baldric, looking more serious than I'd ever seen him.

Repeating after the minister, who looked wildly out of place in his traditional suit and tie, Rogan and I said the words that would bind us for life.

I had bought Rogan a band that matched the one he put on my finger the night he proposed. A simple, wide silver band from a vendor at Windy Springs.

When we kissed, our guests cheered and I could hear Captain Dash shouting, "Huzzah!" over and over through the din. The wind rustled the trees, making the leaves whisper.

It seemed like even the forest itself was congratulating us.

As we walked back down the aisle, hand in hand, I caught a glimpse of blue from the corner of my eye, partially hidden by a tree.

Cordelia.

I gripped Rogan's hand tighter and mouthed the witch's name.

Eyes narrowed, he stopped and stared her down.

Cordelia remained, halfway behind the tree trunk, and slowly raised her arm until she was pointing at me. Then she was gone, as suddenly and mysteriously as she had appeared.

Chills rippled up my spine, leaving gooseflesh in its wake. A painful cramp made its way through my lower abdomen. I pushed myself to keep walking. "She scares me," I whispered to Rogan, as our guests formed a horde behind us and we made our way to the food court for our reception.

Rogan slipped his arm around me, squeezing my waist. "I know, sweetheart. The festival will be done in a couple of weeks, and you won't have to worry about her until next year. Just do your best to stay away from her. And if she approaches you, tell me, okay?"

"If she's so dangerous, why do they let her stay here? Surely, they can get someone else to play the witch." It didn't make sense. Everyone avoided her and warned me away from Cordelia, but she was allowed to keep working at Windy Springs.

"It's not quite that simple. She's… related to the owner."

"Dash?" I hadn't noticed any resemblance between the two of them. In fact, I rarely saw them spending time together or even speaking to one another. It seemed weird that the charming – if mildly insane – pirate captain could be related to the creepy witch. But if Dash was Knowing, that meant the likelihood was good that Cordelia was, too. It evidently ran in families, and I was some bizarre anomaly that hadn't been affected. "Is she—?" I let the question hang in the air.

Rogan picked up on what I hadn't said, and nodded. "She is. She's also his sister."

His sister? "But Dash is so sweet." Sort of. He meant to be sweet. He just came across as—something else, sometimes.

"She's his half-sister, actually. Long story. We can discuss it later. I'd rather talk about us, and what we're going to do with each other tonight." He grinned, green eyes sparkling.

I nodded, and pasted a smile on my face when I heard the shutter of a camera.

It was the happiest day of my life, and some blue-haired witch wasn't going to steal my joy.

I'd worked too hard to find it.

Our honeymoon was us, staying holed up at Rogan's place for four days, and I didn't mind it a bit.

I had plans, and I didn't need to go off on some overpriced trip to put them into motion.

All my life, I'd been waiting.

Waiting for my mother to get her life together. Waiting for Vince to decide I was worth more than his booze.

Waiting to feel loved and accepted for exactly who I was.

Waiting to give the unconditional love I had inside me to someone else. Someone who deserved it.

Waiting.

I was done with that.

Rogan didn't seem too keen on the idea of waiting much longer, either, despite his claims of patience.

We ducked out early from the reception, which was a community potluck much like any other festival evening, with the added benefit of the Rowdy Rennies, a Celtic band, playing onstage.

The fire dancers, Ever and Justice, had made us a cake, which we cut and smashed pieces of into each other's faces before we left.

I had packed enough clothes for the week and had stuck my bag into Rogan's SUV before the ceremony. Now, as we barreled down the expressway toward his house, still in our wedding finery, the anticipation that had been building over the last two weeks had reached its height.

"Excited about tonight?" Rogan asked, one hand snaking across the console to rest on my thigh.

"Excited is probably one word for it," I teased. "I can think of a few other words, as well."

His laughter rumbled, and I smiled.

Humor was one way to deflect the seriousness of our feelings.

"At least we don't have to worry about using birth control," he joked.

"That's true. One disruption off the table," I agreed. "I hope you aren't intimidated by my size."

Rogan flashed me a glance then focused back on the road. "I've never yet encountered a mountain I couldn't climb."

"A *mountain?* Are you trying to spend our first night together lying alone on the couch?"

He flicked the blinker on as he slowed to merge onto the off ramp. "Okay, okay. Maybe 'mountain' wasn't the appropriate word. I'll concede that much."

We were all of five minutes from Rogan's home. *Our* home, though I had yet to feel as though it belonged to me. I'd been bounced around so much in the last several months, *home* wasn't a word I was sure I fully understood the meaning of.

There were things we still needed to work out, like how I could continue working with Layla when I was going to live over an hour away from her now. Or how I would make sure Mim was taken care of. But those were things, Rogan assured me, that we would figure out in time.

Right now, we just needed to focus on us, on our burgeoning relationship.

Rogan pulled into the trailer park and turned down the side street that led to his place. It was barely audible, but I could hear him whistling softly as we got closer.

Once he parked in his drive, he turned the engine off and leaned over the console, lifting my hand and pressing my fingers to his lips.

"We're home, Keisha."

"I think it's a bad idea, Rogan," I said, shaking my head vehemently. "It's not going to work."

"Trust me. Just relax."

It wasn't about relaxing. Or for that matter, trusting him. It was simple common sense.

Rogan was small. I, myself, was not small.

So his idea of carrying me over the threshold and into his trailer was not going to work.

I gritted my teeth. "Just let me walk in like a normal person. It's not like I haven't been here before."

He blocked the door. "You underestimate me, sweetheart." Tucking his chin, he raised his brows at me. "You're my bride. I've waited all my life to do this. It's important to me."

Exasperated, I tried to reason with him. "I understand that, but Rogan, you're too—" I broke off, stopping myself before I said something stupid.

"Too what? Too small? Short? Opposite of strong?" He tapped his foot on the wooden porch.

"I'm sorry." It was dumb to have said it, even if I had been thinking it.

In an instant, he had one arm behind my tailbone, and his other under my knees, scooping me up. "Rogan!" I squealed. "Put me down!"

Kicking the door open with his foot, he carried me inside.

"I'm like, eight inches taller than you are! I'm going to break your damn back!"

I expected he would set me down once we were in, but he didn't. He kept right on walking, carrying me in his strong arms. I was surprised to feel so safe in his grip. He didn't shake a bit, and I finally began to relax.

Maybe I wasn't quite the burden I thought I would be.

"Hmmn, *eight inches* shorter? I think your math is off, m'lady. You're what, five-eight or so?"

We were in the living room, passing the fireplace.

"Yes. Five-eight," I mumbled, as I kept my arms locked around his neck.

"And I'm five-foot-two-and-one-quarter inches. So, you don't have eight inches on me." We'd reached the bedroom door. He kicked it open, and walked slowly across the room to the bed, pouring me out of his arms and onto the mattress.

I had never been so turned on in all my life.

"I'm too small?" he asked, though he smirked as he said it.

"No," I replied, pulling him onto the bed with me. "You are exactly perfect."

His hands went from cradling the sides of my face so he could kiss me, to tangling in my hair. "No more waiting," he said, as his breath began to hitch. He was pressing against me, writhing, gulping air in the fractions of space between kisses.

It'd been so long since I'd felt such intense desire. Even the last year or so I'd been with Vince, between his alcoholism and the emotional abuse, sex been something I did more to appease him, to avoid an argument, than because I wanted it.

The way I wanted it right now.

For Rogan, it had been a matter of years.

Now there was nothing between us, no reason to hold back.

"No more waiting," I agreed, "I need to get this dress off. Help me." Sparks sped through my nerves, lighting fires in locales that had in recent months experienced a drought. I struggled off the bed so Rogan could help me out of my dress. I could feel his fingers trembling as he undid one button at a time.

I wished his first sight of me without clothes didn't have to be when I was so heavy with child. I hadn't been rail-thin before, but I'd been a good deal thinner than I was now. The truth was, I felt self-conscious for my husband to see me for the first time with so much extra weight.

Every insult Vince had ever hurled at me flitted through my mind in that instant. I imagined an eraser in my mind, obliterating every hurtful word he'd flung at me to make me feel inferior.

"I'm done," he whispered, his hands resting on my hips.

I didn't let the dress fall immediately, instead holding it up on my chest, searching for bravery. Despite my desire to be with Rogan, I was finding this part difficult.

I wanted him to see *me,* not this bloated version of me, with extra pounds literally everywhere on my body. In a most shallow sense, I wanted my husband to think me pretty. And quite suddenly, I did not feel at all attractive. I felt like a whale.

"Keisha?"

Rogan.

He had been so patient.

I wanted this. I wanted *him.*

Finally, I turned. Keeping my eyes shut, I let go of my green dress, feeling the soft swish of it as it hit the tops of my bare feet. I heard his sharp intake of breath.

His arms encircled me, and his fingers fumbled with the clasps of my bra. When he managed to get that off, he must have let it drop, because I felt the fabric of it as it brushed against my calf on its way down.

"Look at me, sweetheart," he said, his thumb brushing my cheek.

I stubbornly kept my eyes closed.

"You are so beautiful, Keisha." The tips of his fingers touched me lightly, down my neck, my shoulders, my breasts, pausing on my stomach. "It's hard to believe you're mine. I love you." His voice was thick, burdened with emotion.

Something wet splashed onto my belly, running down it, a tiny river.

My eyes fluttered open, and I watched him as he took the sight of me in. Touching me gently. Reverently. As though I was something precious he was afraid of breaking.

His cheeks were wet, and I brushed the tears from his face. "I love you, Rogan." My heart felt full, as though my chest couldn't possibly withstand the weight of it.

"Your turn," he whispered, stepping out of his boots.

Sliding the sides of his tunic up, I pulled the drawstring of his loose gray pants and then pushed his boxers down with them. In an instant, they met with my green dress on the floor, and we both took a step closer to the bed.

I ran my hands over his shoulders and leaned in to kiss him. Overcome with need, I pushed him back onto the bed, straddling his bare thighs.

"What about the rest of it?" he asked, a smile tugging at his lips as he reached up to twist his fingers in my hair.

"I think we'll leave that on for now. I like it." Running my tongue across my lips, I moved so my mouth was next to his ear. "It's sexy," I whispered.

My knight.

His answering laughter was swallowed up in our passionate kiss as we tumbled together.

Over and again, we came together through the night, drifting to sleep and then waking to join our bodies again.

Eventually, even Rogan's tunic came off, and nothing separated us. Just skin against skin.

I woke early, just as the dim light of dawn was beginning to creep through the curtains, and watched Rogan as he slept. There were creases on his face from the wrinkles in the pillowcase, and he had the sheet pulled up nearly over his head.

There had been so much heartache in his life. So much loss.

But he'd taken that pain and used it to become a better man. A man who worked with kids who needed a steady presence in their lives. A man who'd chosen to not only take a chance on loving me, but who had accepted my child as well.

A child who by all accounts was going to have the same ability Rogan had.

I wondered if this fact would be a hindrance to him, or if it would forge a connection between the two of them.

Rogan reached for me in his sleep and I curled up against him, allowing his arms to hold me tight.

If I thought too much about Knowing, I started to feel like I had bugs crawling in my brain. There was so much I needed to learn about it still. So much I wanted to understand.

I wanted to go back to Mim's and tell her I knew. I wanted information about her, about my mother, and their abilities. That was a conversation that needed to happen before her mind got any foggier. I pushed those worries from my mind, deciding to focus on being present in the moment. Future problems could be dealt with when the future arrived.

Rogan dragged his hand down my side. "Hey." He blinked several times, giving me a sleepy grin. "You're up early."

"I was watching you sleep. And thinking."

"Thinking?" He pulled me even closer, smashing my breasts and stomach against him.

"About us. Family. Knowing."

Pressing his forehead to my chin, he said, "Knowing. Somehow everything always comes back to that."

"We don't have to talk about it today." I wished I hadn't brought it up.

"But we do have to talk about it. Hungry?"

He switched topics so fast, I had to think for a minute before answering. I slid my arm around his neck, pulling his head to rest on my chest, trailing my fingertips down his back. "Yes, actually. I didn't get to eat much at the reception, and I worked up quite an appetite overnight."

"As did I. I'll make you something. You stay here. Save up your strength. You'll need it for later."

"Soon. Just lay here with me for a little longer. I'm enjoying this, just being here with you."

"Are you still sure you made the right choice?" He smiled up at me, his beautiful green eyes sparkling.

He knew what my answer would be.

"Absolutely, Rogan. How about you? Still sure about me?"

"I'm more than sure, sweetheart. You were without a doubt, worth the wait."

I loved Rogan's voice. Thick and heavy, like maple syrup. *Pancakes.* I blinked, shaking the image from my mind. I *was* hungry, but more than that, I ached to have my husband inside me once more.

Breakfast, I decided, could wait a little while longer.

CHAPTER FIFTEEN

Closing day was bittersweet. I had spent three full days a week with most of the Windy Springs people since the beginning of May, and had come to count on many of them as though they were family.

The thought that I wouldn't see them until next spring caused a sharp pain in my chest.

Or maybe it was indigestion. The baby was getting so big, heartburn had become a daily – and sometimes nightly – reality.

There had been a steady trickle of business all day, but the last few weekends in September were always slow, Layla explained. Kids had gone back to school, sports activities started back up, and the lazy weekend days of summer were gone.

Throughout the day, we'd been slowly packing up merchandise, just leaving enough out to draw attention to our shop. Rogan stopped by off and on, for a quick kiss or a feel-up inside the hut.

I remembered back at the beginning of the summer, when Layla and Jack were the ones tumbling out of the hut, clothes and hair askew from an impromptu make-out session. It seemed like such a long time ago. Now Rogan and I were married, and Layla and Jack were still playing at whatever their relationship was supposed to be – spending every available second together during the festival, and reverting to occasional texts over the winter. Weird.

Rogan and I were planning to follow Layla home after closing and spend one night there, so I could pack my things. Other than stopping by to see Mim, there was nothing in that town I was going to miss. I could stop worrying Vince would find me again. Stop looking over my shoulder all the time. Surely, he wouldn't find me at Rogan's.

Rogan and I had plans to make. Furniture and clothes to buy for the baby. A future to look forward to.

It was well past time to stop looking backward.

"I don't want this to end," I said to Layla. "I love being here, in this magical forest." The truth was, I felt safe here. Even though Vince had shown up once, I still felt better surrounded by the trees and a horde of people willing to fight for me.

"I know," she replied. "I feel that way every year when it ends. But there's a group on Facebook for us, so we can all stay in touch with each other. Before we know it, spring will be here again. And next year, we'll have the baby with us." She squealed and clapped her hands. "I can hardly wait. We'll dress the baby up like a tiny little pirate!"

I could hardly wait either, I thought, as I rubbed my aching lower back.

"Ten minutes to closing!" shouted Captain Dash's booming voice. He was walking through his beloved forest, pausing to speak with and hug each vendor. It was well-known throughout the festival that Captain Dash was a little bit off in the head, and most were aware he was Knowing. Though at first, his size and looks were intimidating, he had come to feel like a loveable, eccentric uncle to me, and I was going to miss him over the winter. "Keisha, Layla!"

I braced myself for one of his massive bear hugs.

He lumbered over, embracing Layla and I at the same time, squeezing us against his massive shoulders. "I'll be missing you sweet lasses over the winter."

"I'll miss you too, Captain Dash," I said, and I meant it.

Layla echoed my sentiment.

"You'll call, when the little one comes?" He looked so hopeful, his eyes tender as they met mine.

"I've got your number, Captain," Layla interjected. "We'll call. I promise."

"Good girls. Where's the troll?" he asked, wandering away from us, calling for Gibble.

"Well, that's it," Layla said, as we watched the last of the patrons filing out of the front gates. "I'm going to miss you, Keisha. I had thought you'd be staying with me longer, and I'd get to help with the baby when you first came home. This summer went much different than I expected." She sounded wistful.

"It wasn't what I expected either, Lay. But I'm so happy. And we'll see each other. It's not goodbye yet, we're following you home tonight, remember?"

Suddenly, she buried her face in my chest, throwing her arms around my neck. "I know, but it won't be the same," she mumbled into my shirt.

Patting her back awkwardly, I said, "Nothing ever stays the same, Lay. But you and me, we'll always be best friends. You'll always be auntie to this baby, no matter where I live." God. She was getting me all emotional. "You're being too clingy. Stop." My throat was getting tight, and I pushed her back, averting my gaze. "Let's finish packing."

Rogan showed up a few minutes later, still decked out as Gibble. I reflected for a moment on how thankful I would be to not have to see my husband wearing false yellow teeth in the upcoming months.

The ending of the festival wasn't bringing all sad news, after all.

The lack of that terrible underbite was definitely something to look forward to.

"I don't want to change doctors, not this late in the game," I said, as I helped Rogan set the table for dinner.

Nodding, he put a big bowl of tossed salad on the table. "I agree," he replied. "I think you should stick with Dr. Griffith. We can make the drive once or twice a month until November. Not a big deal at all."

I put out our silverware and sat, as Rogan plopped a steak onto first my plate, then his, and took his own seat.

I waited as he closed his eyes and did his silent prayer thing. "This is great, Rogan. Thanks for cooking tonight." It *was* good. To be honest, Rogan was a better cook than I, though my meals were usually passable.

"Glad you like it." He smiled around a forkful of food.

"My only worry is me going into labor and not being able to get to the hospital on time." The truth was, it was more than just a worry. I'd started obsessing over the possibility, imagining in terrible detail giving birth alone on the side of the road, unable to reach Rogan or anyone else to help.

It was making for some fantastic nightmares.

"We'll head there as soon as you feel a contraction, I promise. If it turns out to be false, we'll visit Mim or Layla instead." He winked at me, popping another bite of steak into his mouth.

It was when he said things like this, reassuring me he was always going to be there for me, that I felt a rush of emotion for him so strong, I wasn't sure I could contain it. "I love you, Rogan," I said simply. There weren't enough words to encompass the way I felt for him. The simple ones would have to do.

"And I love you, sweetheart. I don't want you to worry. Whatever happens, I'll be there with you."

"I know you will." I set my fork down on my plate. Again, I remembered something that had been bothering me, a niggling thought which had popped into my brain unbidden at the most inopportune times. I had hoped Rogan would have brought it up by now, but he hadn't.

And I needed to know.

I cleared my throat. "I have a question," I said.

He waited, his eyes on mine. "Go ahead."

This seemed harder than I thought it would be. Best to just get out with it, I guessed. "Rogan." I swallowed hard, pushing down the lump in my throat. "What did you do to Vince?" Though my voice had started out the question strong, it ended on a whisper.

He took in a deep breath and held it in his cheeks, drumming his fingers on the table. Then he blew the breath out. "I did tell you we could talk about this. I guess now is as good a time as any. Are you sure you don't want to finish eating first?"

He constantly tried to get me to eat. It was sweet. But the bigger the baby got, the less room there seemed to be for my stomach. Little bites, little meals. That's all I could handle lately.

Instead of saying no, I just shook my head.

Rogan patted his mouth with a napkin. Pat, pat, pat.

Clearly buying time.

My real question burst from me, "Is he dead?"

I had considered the possibility multiple times and felt surprisingly okay with it. I knew that was wrong. I *knew* it was and yet, I couldn't stop myself from feeling that way. He'd hurt me and threatened me, abused me both mentally and physically. I wasn't able to summon any compassion or empathy toward him. If Rogan and the other guys from Windy Springs had actually "taken care of" Vince the way I thought, it would be one less thing I needed to worry about. One less thing to be afraid of.

Maybe that made me a terrible person. Or maybe it made me a protective mother.

Obviously startled, Rogan made a noise that sounded like a cross between a cough and a hiccup. "What? Dead?"

I rushed on, "Because it would be okay. I wouldn't be mad."

"That's good to know, I suppose. No, Keisha. He's not dead. At least, he wasn't the last time I saw him." Clutching his napkin again, he started mopping at his forehead. He'd broken out in a sweat.

I didn't feel any better, hearing Vince was alive. I didn't feel anything for him at all.

"What then? Where is he? Do I need to be worried?"

Rogan was drinking his bottled water at an alarming pace. 'Gulping' would be a more accurate term than 'drinking'. Sooner or later, he was going to run out of ways to stall.

I tapped my foot on the kitchen floor, waiting for an answer.

"You remember there was a fight."

"Yes..." I nodded, encouraging him to go on.

"Eventually, we caught him. Vince was... unhappy about that." Rogan shook his head, as though recalling the struggle of that day. "Jason – the security guy, remember? – he helped. Along with Jack, Dash, and me. Vince was angry and violent, which you already know, I imagine. And just determined to find you. Bugger clawed my face..."

His voice trailed off for a minute.

"When he hit me, he was yelling things, saying what he was going to do when he found you. How he wanted to hurt you." Dropping the napkin, he balled his hands into fists. Dark pink flushed his cheeks. "I *wanted* to kill him," he stated it in a flat, detached voice.

I'd never heard him speak like this before, and it left me feeling mildly nauseated.

"I wanted to. And I could have. Believe me, Keisha. Don't doubt that I could have killed him." Pinching the bridge of his nose, he squeezed his eyes shut as he took several deep breaths. "But taking the life of another human being is a heavy burden to bear."

The way he said it made an icy lump form in my chest. It was like he knew about it firsthand.

He pressed his hands flat on the table. Rogan was almost constantly moving his hands, I had noticed.

"So. Jason and I... subdued Vince. Jack and Dash and I talked it out, while Jason kept him down. You remember when I told you I could use Knowing to force different thoughts into someone's mind? If I focused my ability with those of others like me?"

I nodded, working in my mind to comprehend his words. I felt as though we were in a race, and he was miles ahead of me, running, while I waddled along, no hope of ever catching up.

"That's basically what we did. We tied him up, put him in the backseat of his own truck, and drove him out about thirty miles to the west. Jack and Dash followed in Jack's vehicle. The three of us erased a few things from his mind."

"Erased." It was all I could manage. The whole thing sounded unbelievable.

"Right. I want you to understand, this is not a thing that's done often, or done lightly. Emergencies only, which this was. Dash and I decided it was the only way to keep you safe, and Jack agreed. We took only the memories from just before he saw you at Wendy's – that's how he found you, he followed us that day from Wendy's, after we went to your doctor appointment. Remember that black truck? That was Vince – so he couldn't remember where to find you. I wanted to erase all his memories of you, but that wouldn't have been ethical, and this power, we must use it appropriately. There are… guidelines." He paused, pursed his lips. "Anyway. Dash held him still, and we sorted through his mind, taking everything from about two days before the day at Wendy's until the day he showed up at the festival." Now he was rubbing his head, the fingers on both hands locked together, dragging over and back, over and back, across his scalp.

Thoughts banged around in my head, vying for attention. Vince used to drive a big Buick from the late nineties. When had he gotten this black truck? Had he switched cars specifically so he could follow me?

Rogan's eyes never strayed from mine.

I wanted to say something reassuring; it was obvious his actions had distressed him.

I wanted to tell him it was all right, I didn't mind. Minutes before, I'd told him it would have been okay with me if he'd killed my ex-boyfriend. The father of my baby. And I'd meant it, too.

Somehow, thinking that Rogan had killed Vince in the heat of struggle, when Vince was clearly intent on harming me, was easier to think of than what he'd actually done.

My throat felt suddenly dry, and my hand trembled a bit as I lifted a glass of water to my lips.

I could forgive him murder because he would have done it without thinking. It would have happened in a split second, Rogan fighting to keep me and the baby safe. He would have been protecting me. But this was different. He had calculated, along with other men, to do this... this *thing* he had the power to do. It seemed sinister, almost. Bile bubbled up in my throat, leaving a horrid, acidic flavor on my tongue.

Though he'd been open with me about it, had in fact offered me the chance to walk away from it, I had chosen to accept him, aware he was Knowing. Aware of the things he could do.

At the time, it had all seemed so detached from us. When I trailed my fingers over his bare skin, or he held me at night in his strong, warm arms, this thing, this ability he had didn't feel as though it touched our relationship. It seemed far away, like knowing Scotland existed somewhere *over there* but also knowing I'd never see it in person.

Now, I suddenly felt as though it had risen up and sucker punched me in the face. I found I was unprepared for the searing pain of it.

I took another drink of water and it sat uncomfortably in my throat. I had to fight to force it down.

My husband, the man I slept beside every night, could do this. He could worm his way into another person's mind and take memories out. He could shift existing memories around. He could communicate with the dead, or the nearly dead.

He could do this to *me.* He could get inside my brain and fiddle with my private thoughts. My memories. Had he ever peeked into my brain? Would I know it if he had?

How many times had he felt he had the justification to do this? To rummage around in someone's mind? Steal things? What were the guidelines? Was there some sort of threshold that constituted the emergency use of that ability?

All at once, it seemed so real. I felt sweaty and nauseated.

"I feel sick," I said stupidly.

The look of personal distress on Rogan's face changed to one of concern. For me. Hurrying around the table, he helped me stand. "It's too much for you to take in, and I'm sorry, sweetheart. I shouldn't have put it all out like that. Let's get you lying down. You should rest."

Rest? Would I ever relax again? In that moment, I thought I might spend the rest of my life wondering if my husband was mentally invading my privacy.

He tucked me in on the couch, a thick fleece blanket covering me. He took a few quick steps backward to turn on the electric fireplace. Seconds later, he was lifting my head so he could slide beneath it, leaving my head and shoulders resting on his thighs.

We remained there in utter silence for what felt like an hour. I turned on my side, watching the flames flicker in the fireplace.

Rogan had one hand on my shoulder, and the other playing with my hair. He spoke first, "Still love me?" he asked. It was obvious he was trying to keep his tone light and silly.

"Of course, I love you," I replied automatically. I had no doubt about that. I needed to force myself to come to terms with his abilities.

Soon enough, I'd have a child with those same abilities. Pushing thoughts of it away wouldn't help my child. I needed to know everything about it, so I could teach the baby when the time came. "I'm trying, Rogan. It's going to take me time to understand it all." Over and over, his fingers slid through my hair. "It's just— there's so much."

"I know, sweetheart. And I hate to tell you this, but there is so much still I need to tell you. I need to know you don't hate me for what I've done. I did what I had to do to keep you safe. I don't regret it, but I do wish it hadn't been necessary."

"How many times have you done this? Erased someone's memories?" A big part of me wanted him to say it'd been the only time. And he would never do it again.

"I don't keep track, sweetheart. I need you to trust me that it's only done when necessary, and leave it at that." His hand in my hair had slowed to nearly a stop, and then picked up its pace again.

Turning onto my back, so I could look up at him, I reached up to touch his face.

His face was so dear to me.

I could do this. *We* could do this. Together.

"Promise me you won't ever do that to me. I don't want you rummaging around in my brain, taking things out."

Rogan smiled then, but it was a sad, heavy smile, as though the burden he'd been made to carry was far too much. "I promise."

The baby was awake, kicking, rolling around inside me.

Taking Rogan's hand, I placed it on my belly. Together, we watched with amazement as my t-shirt shifted with the baby's movements.

"I'll hold you to that," I said.

"I always keep the promises I make, Keisha," he replied.

With all my heart, I wanted to believe him.

CHAPTER SIXTEEN

November 2010

"Are you sure?"

He'd asked me that question when we had first decided to move forward with our relationship, and at the time, I had found it endearing.

Now, it just pissed me off.

I gripped the corner of the wall, clenching my teeth together, as if it would somehow relieve the pain ricocheting through my abdomen and lower back. When it began to ease up, I shot him a look.

If looks could kill, I would have been a widow.

"I don't *know,* Rogan, I've never been in labor before! How could I be sure?" I had wakened that morning with lower back pain, and put it down to the way the baby was sitting. After several hours, the back pain moved around to my hips, and then began to shoot across my abdomen in pulsing, agonizing waves.

The waves of pain had been coming every eight minutes for the last half an hour.

"I think we'd better go," Rogan said now, rushing around the trailer. In less than two minutes, he'd gotten the bag I had packed, my purse, and a thick fleece blanket out into his SUV. Darting back to where I stood clutching the wall, he helped me get my coat and shoes on.

Once I was in the passenger seat, Rogan buckled my seatbelt for me and then tenderly tucked the blanket around me.

It was cold outside. Freezing. Four inches of snow had already fallen so far, with at least three more to come, if the weathermen were on the ball.

My teeth chattered, but whether it was from the pain or the temperatures, I didn't know.

"We'll get there in time. It's okay," Rogan said, though I thought he might be talking to himself.

He fumbled with the car keys, trying and failing to get them into the slot. His hands were shaking. "We'll make it, we'll make it," he said, so softly I barely heard him. Finally, the engine roared to life.

I wished I felt as certain as he was. The contractions were awful, and it was difficult to imagine them getting worse and closer together, though I knew they would. I wasn't sure I could bear it.

Images of the dreams I'd been having, of giving birth alone on the side of the road, flashed through my mind.

Fear blasted through me, nonsensical though it was. I wasn't alone, I reminded myself. I had Rogan.

Everything would be okay. He had promised me that.

"I'm not sure I can make it," I whimpered as we sailed down the expressway. "I don't think I can."

"Of course you can, sweetheart," he assured me.

I fixed my eyes on the green numbers of the SUV's digital clock.

It had been six minutes since the last contraction, and I could already feel my abdominal muscles tightening, gearing up for another round of agony. I tried to remember the breathing exercises I'd learned in my birthing classes.

I closed my eyes, forcing myself to remember the breathing exercises. Forcing myself to notice other things around me, sounds and sensations and anything else that wasn't related to the pain.

We hit a pothole. The SUV bounced. I screamed in agony.

Rogan began to whistle.

"One, two, three, four," Rogan counted, his mouth pressed against my ear.

He held my hand.

I held my breath.

"Again," Dr. Griffith said.

I gulped air and kept it tight in my chest as I pushed.

It was never going to end. I'd been too far dilated for pain meds when we'd finally gotten to the hospital, even though I demanded them in a high-pitched, hysterical sort of voice. I was doing all the things the doctor instructed and yet, the misery continued to ricochet throughout my body and I was certain my hips were actually shattering.

Why would any woman willingly do this more than once?

"You've got this, sweetheart, you've got this," Rogan whispered.

I couldn't hold my breath any longer. I couldn't push any longer.

Was there any way the doctor could make it stop, if I promised to come back tomorrow? I would have asked, if there had been any way I could form words, but there wasn't.

"Keep going, keep going," Dr. Griffith commanded.

A sudden lightness swept through me, as though I'd been relieved of a great burden. Which, technically, I guess I had.

Dr. Griffith was saying things, and Rogan was saying things, and the nurse was talking away, but it all sounded like background noise. Radio static.

My eyes were only focused on the space between my knees. Dr. Griffith was hunched over, and I could feel things going on down there, unfamiliar sensations I couldn't lay claim to with any words I knew.

Time seemed to freeze, and then all at once it was moving again. Now noise surrounded me, and Rogan was saying, "You did it, sweetheart," over and over, and Dr. Griffith was laying my baby on my chest.

"Congratulations. Beautiful little girl you've got here," he said, before turning to speak to the nurse.

She didn't cry.

"Is she okay?" I asked his retreating form. Despite what Rogan had told me about the feeling of foreboding being common in mothers carrying a child with Knowing, it still bothered me. I could accept that my baby had this weird ability. I just needed someone to tell me for sure that otherwise, she was fine. Cradling the baby in my arms, I looked up at Rogan. "Is she okay?" I asked him.

How would he know? I just wanted someone to say it out loud, so I could be certain.

Besides, sometimes Rogan *did* know things that other people didn't.

"She's perfect, Keisha." Tears were streaming down his cheeks, and he didn't bother to wipe them away.

Rogan had said it. It must be true.

With this treasure of knowledge tucked safely into my heart, I allowed myself to sink into the delirium of joy sweeping through me.

She was here. She was safe. She was perfect.

Rogan kept kissing the top of my head, telling me he loved me.

Cupping the blanket around her shoulders and wobbly head, I took the first good, hard look at my baby.

Wisps of black hair. Tiny red mouth, shaped almost like a heart. Long arms and legs, like me.

The baby looked back at me with piercing, purple eyes.

For the first time in many years, I began to weep.

In The Presence Of Knowing

"You don't have to do this," I said for the umpteenth time.

"Yes, I do." Rogan picked the pen up off the side table next to my hospital bed.

We were filling out the forms for the birth certificate.

"I can give her my maiden name. Lawson." My top teeth bit into my bottom lip. I twisted the sheet in my fist.

Leaning over me until we were nearly nose to nose, Rogan asked, "Do *you* want her to have your maiden name?"

The truth was, I didn't. I wanted her to have our last name, O'Connor. But telling my husband that felt like pushing a burden on him he might not be ready to bear. I wanted to know *he* wanted it.

Rogan sighed, sitting carefully on the edge of my bed. "Sweetheart, it's not like I didn't know you were pregnant when we got together. I knew what I was taking on. I want to be with you. I want to raise this child with you. I want for us to be a family." Pausing to gaze at the sleeping baby in her plastic bassinet, he wiped at his eyes with the back of his hand. When he spoke again, his voice was much quieter, "I want her last name to be mine."

"She doesn't even have a first name yet." I knew for sure what I wasn't going to do. No more names beginning with 'K'. Breaking that tradition was my first stab at being a different, better parent than the women who had gone before me in my family.

Firsts.

There'd been a lot of firsts over the last year. Most of them had been good ones. Some of them had been life-changing. First time working at Windy Springs Renaissance Festival. First time living away from my hometown.

A smile spread across my face.

First time sleeping with a troll.

My first baby. And just like that, her name popped into my head.

"Eve," I said out loud.

"What?"

"Her name. Eve. Evie." She might want something more adult when she got older. What names could I shorten up to Eve? "How about Evelyn?"

"Evelyn," Rogan repeated. "I like that. Middle name?"

I considered the options. My middle name was Lynnae, but I had never been overly fond of it. I spent a few seconds trying to morph Rogan's name into something feminine, then gave up, latching onto a new idea. He was a good man. He had given me so much. I wanted to give him something in return.

"What was your mother's name?"

"Faith," he answered automatically. "Why?"

"I think Evelyn Faith has a good ring to it."

"Evelyn Faith O'Connor," he said, grinning like an idiot. "Our daughter."

CHAPTER SEVENTEEN

March 2011

"She hardly ever cries," I explained to the pediatrician.

She gave me a look that said she thought I might have dropped my marbles on the way in to her office. "You made an appointment to complain that your baby doesn't cry enough? I've got to tell you, that's a new one for me."

"I mean, that's not normal, is it?" I held Evie against my shoulder as I swayed back and forth in the tiny exam room, gently patting her back, hoping to get a burp out of her. "Babies are supposed to cry." I had read plenty of books on new motherhood. There were lots of tips for managing on minimal sleep, how to get your partner to help more, and ways to cope when your baby wouldn't stop crying.

But Evie didn't really cry. What she did do was catch my gaze and stare intently at me, sometimes so intently that I had to look away. It was disturbing, like she could see inside me, see my soul.

When she heard Rogan's voice, she would lift her little head and turn until she found his face, locking her purple eyes with his green ones.

The two of them spent a good deal of time doing that. Staring at each other.

It creeped me out.

"Consider yourself a very lucky mother, Keisha. I'll check her out, but I'm sure she's fine."

I knew she was tired of me coming in so often, but I couldn't help it. Being responsible for Evie's life was scary. And she was sick a lot.

The pediatrician waved that off, too. Babies had weak immune systems, she said. Being in public often, they could easily pick up germs. The average infant had six to eight colds a year.

But Evie seemed to be chronically sick. Green stuff coming out of her nose. Coughing. Ear infections. My five-month-old infant had already developed an allergy to one class of antibiotics, she'd been on them so often.

Besides, I rarely took Evie out in public. Rogan taught his classes at night. I stayed home with the baby, creating wings for Layla while Evie slept.

Since she picked up colds so easily, I made anyone who wanted to visit remove their shoes and wash their hands and arms up to their elbows before they could hold her.

"Her eyes are so pretty," the doctor said, as she peered into Evie's nose with her little light. "Who does she get those from? Must be recessive."

Mine were brown. Rogan's were green. I was sure she was fishing for a tidbit of explanation, which was none of her business.

"My mother and grandmother both have purple eyes," I explained. "Runs in my family."

A lot more than that runs in my family, I thought.

"I see," she replied politely, but the tone of her voice held a question in it.

Why was it any of her business if my husband was Evie's biological father? Rogan was there, changing diapers, rocking her, setting alarms at night so we didn't forget to wake up and give her the next dose of antibiotics.

Rogan *was* her father.

Vince seemed like such a faded memory, I could almost make myself believe he had never existed.

"Looks like she's got the beginnings of another ear infection, so it's back on antibiotics. Otherwise, she seems just fine, Keisha.

Try not to worry. Your next baby will likely be a screamer to make up for how good Evie is."

I knew she was trying to joke with me, but I was only further irritated. "All right, thanks." Scooping Evie up in my arms, I accepted the paper prescription the doctor handed me, and headed out the door.

Back to the pharmacy we went. I felt like we should be racking up some kind of frequent flyer miles for free prizes, as often as we were there.

My body was beginning to feel normal again. I realized how much I had missed wearing pants that had zippers and snaps while I'd been pregnant. The extra weight was coming off slowly but surely.

Rogan was enjoying the fact that I was more flexible than I had been when we were first married.

He was enjoying that a lot. To be perfectly honest, so was I.

Where our initial lovemaking had been cumbersome and cautious, now that my body had recovered from childbirth, it was, for lack of a better word, *hot.*

Rogan had just come home from work, sweaty and evidently sore from another evening teaching kids who were not entirely cooperative how to defend themselves and maintain strength and balance. Some of the kids were serious about what they were learning. Some of them had a tendency to kick Rogan in the shins when he wasn't looking. But all the kids loved Rogan. I'd sat in on his classes a couple of times over the winter, and it was easy to see how desperate these children were for the attention of a caring adult. They clung to him, clamored to be listened to, held on to his legs as he tried to walk out at the end of the night.

For a change, I'd taken off my sturdy nursing bra in favor of a new, lacy black one that kept the girls up where they needed to be. I undid the first four buttons of my shirt, which I had paired with a set of form-fitting blue jeans. My long hair, freshly washed and dried, was a big, fluffy mess. I hadn't gone lightly with the eye liner or red lipstick.

"Hi," I said softly, as Rogan came through the door.

"Hi," he answered as he put his bags into the front closet. Turning around and getting a good look at me, he paused. "I mean, *hello*. What's all this for?" He was in front of me in an instant, touching my hair, sliding his hands over my shoulders. Down my arms.

Cupping my ass.

"Baby's asleep," I said. "She should be out for a while. You got any energy left, teacher?"

"You know, I think I might have a little yet on reserve." He cocked his head to the side, like he was thinking hard about it. "Yeah, in fact, I do. I feel it, right down here." He took my hand, guiding it to the very apparent 'burst of energy' between his legs.

"You should save your energy. Let me help you undress," I teased, as I tugged his t-shirt up and over his head, tossing it onto the floor. "That's more like it." Pressing against him, I slid my fingertips through the dark hair on his chest and sighed. "I've been waiting for this all day."

"You and me both, sweetheart."

The harder and more fervently he kissed me, the farther away the bedroom seemed to be.

The living room floor was much closer, and before I knew it, we were horizontal in front of the electric fireplace, its flames creating flickering shadows across our bare skin as we moved together.

Rogan flipped me on top of him, his strong hands caressing my lower back as I enjoyed his burst of energy.

"It occurs to me," I whispered in his ear, "that I might be more like Mim than I thought I was."

He stopped moving abruptly. "What?" Scrunching his nose, he focused in on me. "Huh?" His breathing was fast and shallow, his face flushed with excitement.

I trailed the side of his face with my finger. "I was just thinking, I do really like me a nice Irish boy."

His laughter, low and rumbly, skittered across my skin like sparks of electricity. "Is that so? Let me show you what all a nice Irish boy can do, lass."

He proceeded to do just that, and I was fighting within myself to keep quiet, to not scream out, though everything inside me wanted to roar with desire. Don't wake the baby, I thought. Don't wake the baby up.

Rogan said my name, squeezing my shoulders. "Keisha," he said, sounding distraught. "Keisha, stop."

Stop? What did he mean, stop? I couldn't stop, not right that second. "Almost," I gasped, grinding against him. "I'm almost there."

With more force than he'd ever used against me, Rogan shoved me off him, leaping to his feet and leaving me lying on the floor, naked, confused and feeling more than a little bit rejected.

"Rogan?"

But he didn't answer me, because he was running to the bedroom.

The bedroom, where Evie was sleeping.

Dread replaced the feeling of rejection as I jumped up to follow him.

"What is it? What's the matter?" I hadn't heard her cry. Well, of course I hadn't. Evie never cried.

When I rounded the corner into the bedroom, Rogan had Evie in his arms.

She looked so still, so small, and ice settled into my chest, stopping me from taking a breath.

Rogan was somber, tipping his head so he could put his ear to Evie's chest.

A bizarre sound like radio static echoed through the room.

Is she breathing? I wanted to ask him, but I didn't want to hear the answer. I just stood there, staring.

"We have to go, Keisha." He had Evie cradled in one arm as if he was holding a football, and with the opposite hand he put her car seat up on our bed, moving the straps out of the way so he could fit the baby in.

My teeth began to chatter.

"Go?" I repeated stupidly.

"To the hospital. Get dressed." He was brisk now, quickly moving about the room. The baby was in her seat, Rogan was dressed. He was stuffing his wallet in his back jeans pocket.

I still stood just inside the doorway, naked. Shivering. Unable to move. Unable to think.

Was my baby dying?

Why was I naked while my baby was dying?

"Keisha!" he barked at me. "Get dressed!"

The power in his voice shook me from my stupor and I moved awkwardly, robotically, lifting yesterday's t-shirt from the floor and slipping it on. Pants. I needed pants. Did I have pants? Where were they?

Rogan disappeared into the living room, reappearing seconds later with the jeans I had slid off with such anticipation less than an hour before. He pushed me onto the bed, putting my feet into the leg holes and yanking them up my legs. Standing me on my feet, he finished pulling them up, snapping and zipping them for me.

Grabbing Evie's car seat, he ran to the SUV and buckled her in.

I followed, wondering how my legs were moving when I couldn't even feel them.

The strange, radio static-like sound had followed us into the vehicle.

We were halfway to the hospital when I found I could speak again. "Is she breathing?" Of course, she was breathing.

Of course she was. She was fine. She was perfect.

Rogan had promised me that the day she'd been born.

She hadn't looked like she was breathing.

"She's breathing, but she's not breathing right."

How had he heard her? *I* was her mother. *I* should have heard her.

His voice sounded cracked. Broken.

Broken like everything inside me would be, if Evie were to —

"How did you know?"

We were almost at the hospital. Just one more turn and we'd be there. Someone would help us.

Why hadn't we called an ambulance?

"I just... knew."

Guilt slithered over me, making me shiver even harder.

"Did you hear her? I didn't hear anything." I'd been busy, trying not to cry out in the throes of passion.

Don't wake the baby up, I had thought.

While Evie had been in her bassinet, gasping for air.

"Keisha. I didn't hear her. I just knew. I... I felt it. In my mind. This is not your fault. You didn't fail."

He knew me. Knew what I was thinking.

Rogan knew everything, apparently.

We were in the emergency room lot. Rogan came around and opened my door, then the one to the backseat, fussing with the car seat.

I waited as he got Evie out.

Waiting, always waiting. I'm a star at that game.

"Keisha!" he shouted.

Then I stumbled toward him, feeling clammy and cold and like I was about to throw up.

He clutched Evie to his chest as he spun around from the backseat, frantic. His green eyes met mine, and in them I could see pure terror. Agony. "Go, we have to go!"

The doors of the emergency room seemed ridiculously far away as we ran through the lot. Rogan had tossed a blanket over Evie, and the corners of it fluttered in the wind. It was snowing, fat white flakes falling on us, sticking to my eyelashes, my lips. The freezing wind bit at me, but the cold I felt was coming from inside my bones.

As we burst into the emergency room, I was certain I would never be warm again.

"Somebody help us!" Rogan shouted. "Our baby isn't breathing!"

People were moving, shouting, yanking Evie from Rogan's arms.

The twin scents of antiseptic and blood were heavy in the air.

We followed along behind them, like puppets being pulled on a string. Rogan was jogging and getting farther and farther ahead of me. My speed kept slowing down, despite my efforts. Reaching out, I tried calling Rogan's name, but no sound emerged from my lips. The lights were bright, way too bright, and they kept getting brighter.

Brighter and bigger until they were all I could see.

The floor came up to greet me, and everything went black.

CHAPTER EIGHTEEN

"Tracheomalacia," the doctor rolled the word off his tongue like it wasn't a six-syllable linguistic riddle.

"Trach... trach?" I gave up, turning my failed effort instead into a question.

It was just past six in the morning, and I was guiltily nursing a bottle of Mountain Dew. I hadn't slept since we'd brought Evie in the night before. My gut clenched at the memory and I gripped the bottle tighter in my hands. Last night had been a haze of confusion and fear. My head still felt sore from hitting it on the shiny hospital floor when I passed out. There had been a rush of activity around Evie, medical personnel pushing Rogan and me away as they worked.

I had been desperate to know why Evie hadn't been breathing right.

Now the doctor was giving me an answer, and I couldn't even pronounce it.

"Here, sit." Dr. Towers indicated the two recliners next to the crib where Evie slept, with Rogan curled up possessively around her tiny body. An oxygen tent was over the crib to help her breathe. I had tried climbing in there with her when we first got into the room, but my height made it next to impossible. Rogan fit just fine.

We sat, after Towers dragged the second chair closer to me, so we were knee to knee.

"You know what a trachea is?" He was watching my face, waiting to see my reaction.

Of course, I knew what a trachea was. It's… it's the part of the neck the doctors in television shows cut and stick a pen into when a person isn't breathing. I nodded, waving vaguely at my own neck, under my chin.

I wished fervently I had all my brain cells functioning for this conversation. I wanted to understand what was going on with my daughter, but the lack of sleep was making me slow and stupid.

Dr. Towers took my wrist, guiding my hand down a little lower on my neck. "There."

"Okay."

Dropping my hand, he formed his pointer fingers and thumbs into two circles, stacking them atop one another. "Basically, your trachea is a series of rings. The scope showed that Evelyn's trachea is underdeveloped." He paused, looking hard into my eyes to make sure I was following.

I nodded, then took several gulps of my caffeinated high fructose corn syrup laden beverage.

Hours before, they'd done something called a bronchoscopy on Evie. "The scope", he'd called it.

"So her trachea is floppy. When she gets sick, like she is now, the trachea sort of… bends over, creating that strange sound you were hearing."

"Like radio static." This was good, because I could understand these words. Short, simple words. I bounced my head up and down again. "What do we do?" A plan of action meant there was something I could do to fix this. Fix Evie.

"Mostly, we wait. Most kids with tracheomalacia outgrow it sometime in toddlerhood. The situation corrects itself with time. In the interim, you'll need to be careful when she gets sick with any kind of respiratory illness. Once she's stable enough to go home, we'll get you set up with a nebulizer, and we'll have a respiratory therapist come down and teach you how to use it."

I was going to need a lot more Mountain Dew. Maybe even go back to hitting the energy drinks. I'd been trying to stay off the caffeine while I was breastfeeding, but desperate times and all that.

"Many kids with tracheomalacia also develop asthma, so that's something to watch for as well."

Asthma. That wasn't a foreign word. I could manage that.

He stood, settling a hand on my shoulder. "I know it sounds frightening, but she'll be okay. We'll talk again before she goes home, Mrs. O'Connor."

I'd been about to thank him, but my mouth froze when the door to our room banged open.

Captain Dash barged in, his enormous presence outfitted in loose black pants and his typical puffy white pirate shirt. Several long gold chains hung around his neck. Leather boots reached his knees. A red bandanna was tied around his long golden dreadlocks.

He went straight for Dr. Towers.

"You'll tell me what's happened with my goddaughter." True to his persona, he barked the order at the doctor, as though he was a lowly servant on Dash's ship.

And... wait. His goddaughter? What? When had that happened?

"Captain Dash, ssshh." I put my finger to my lips, tipping my head toward the crib where Rogan and Evie slept.

Dr. Towers seemed startled.

How could I explain the presence of this loud, enormous pirate in my daughter's hospital room? Sighing, I introduced him. "Dr. Towers, I'd like you to meet my boss, Dashiel Winston."

Eyes darting from me, to Dash, and back to me again as though he was waiting for the punchline to a joke, Dr. Towers stuck his hand out to Dash, grasping it and shaking gently. "Glad to meet you, Mr. Winston."

Dash clamped his opposite hand over the top of their joined hands, holding tight. "It's Captain."

Dr. Towers narrowed his eyes and shot me a confused look.

I shrugged, helpless. What could I do?

"Uh, Captain Winston," he amended. "I was just explaining Evelyn's diagnosis to Mrs. O'Connor. Perhaps she can fill you in, as I've got rounds to make this morning." He fought to rip his hand from Dash's death grip.

"Keisha," Dash said, turning to me as the doctor – if not ran, walked at a much faster than normal pace – from the room. "What's happened to our darling lass?"

Chucking my empty pop bottle into the trash, I picked up my purse. "Let me get a drink from the vending machine quick, and then I'll fill you in, Captain."

"But she'll be okay," I finished.

It was still early but the sun had risen, illuminating Evie's room, though Rogan still snored away with the baby in the tent-covered crib.

"There's a relief, isn't it? Layla called Jack last night and Jack called me right away, of course."

Of course? Dash was like a bull, determined to push his way right into the china shop and make it his new home.

I hadn't moved the chairs from when I'd been speaking to Dr. Towers, so they were still shoved close together as Dash and I talked.

"It must have been so frightening for you." He looked genuinely concerned, and my heart softened toward him despite his bordering-on-rude insistence that he had some role in my life beyond that of a seasonal boss. Apparently overcome with emotion, he launched forward and enveloped me in one of his bone-crushing hugs.

My head was forced down, against his massive chest, and that's when I saw the bulge in his pants.

What the…?

I struggled to release myself from his embrace. Sure, Dash was attractive – okay, he was more than attractive, he was probably the pirate crush of every lustful wench – but one, I was married and two, he wasn't mentally stable. So whatever he was thinking, coming here, wrapping his arms around me under the guise of caring for my daughter...

"Captain Dash, I—" I broke off, watching in amazement as the bulge began to wiggle, then moved entirely, under his pocket and then up toward the waist of his pants.

The hem of his shirt trembled, and a great rumble of a laugh escaped him as he released me and sat back. Cupping his hand and slipping it under his shirt, he drew it out and held it toward me.

"Little fella must have been hiding in my pocket this morning."

I stared at his empty hand, up to his face, back to his hand.

Clearly, I had seen... *something* move. I blinked and rubbed my eyes. I was also exhausted and under a great deal of emotional stress.

Maybe I just needed sleep.

"How nice," I said, for lack of anything else coming to mind. Clearing my throat, I went on, "I'm sure Rogan will be waking up soon."

Please, please, Rogan, wake up soon.

Like magic, my husband sat up in the crib, smiling sleepily at me. Then he saw Dash, and moved around to face us, careful not to disturb Evie.

Grateful for the excuse to move away from Captain Dash and his weird wiggling bulges and empty hand, I rushed to the crib and unzipped the tent to let Rogan out.

The two men hugged, and it surprised me as it always did, how tiny Rogan looked against Dash, who kept his supposedly full hand out to the side.

"Thanks for coming, Captain," Rogan said. "Means a lot to us."

As they stepped apart, Dash held his hand out to Rogan.

I watched carefully for his reaction.

"Aww," Rogan said. "What's he doing here?" My husband stuck his finger out, tickling the imaginary something in Dash's hand.

That was cool, then. Maybe the extra oxygen in the room was causing some kind of bizarre group hallucination.

"Hitched a ride, my guess. Stowaway."

My energy drink can was empty. How had that happened? "Rogan," I whispered. "Do you see something there?"

He was practically oozing a "goochiegoochiegoo" vibe. "Oh, right. I forgot."

Forgot what? I shook my head, hoping the action might dislodge something that made sense.

"Sweetheart, remember when you thought the forest had rats?"

I shivered, vividly recalling the feeling of rodents scurrying over my feet at Windy Springs.

Rogan flattened his palm, holding it out next to Dash's. Then he spun around to me, holding his palm up toward me. "Touch it," he commanded.

"No." Last night and this morning had been weird enough. I didn't want to be touching imaginary things in my husband's hand.

"Come on. Seriously, Keisha. He's not going to hurt you. I promise."

With my pointer finger, I hesitantly poked the air just above Rogan's palm. I nearly screamed when I felt something furry.

Hallucinations couldn't be—furry.

"What *is* that?" I yanked my hand back, wiping it on my jeans.

"It's a mudgen." Rogan grinned, green eyes sparkling.

Sure, *his* eyes could sparkle. He'd gotten hours of sleep.

"A… mudgen. Of course."

"Think of it as a baby chipmunk."

"An invisible baby chipmunk. Why not?" If I could just get some sleep, or maybe more caffeine, it might make sense. As it stood, I felt like I was falling through that old movie, Fantasia, surrounded by bizarre, nonsensical things.

Dash was looking through the crib's tent, staring at Evie, his face pressed against the thin fabric. Whispering.

"They're creatures of our forest. They are protectors, sometimes signaling when danger is around. If you feel them scurrying around you, be extra aware of your surroundings. But in general, they are friendly."

"Can—can you see them? Because I don't see anything." Another impossible thing I was being asked to believe. But I recalled how often I felt the little rodents when Cordelia came near. Maybe they had been trying to warn me.

"I can. Probably anyone Knowing can. It's just another piece of the veil, lifted for our eyes."

Sometimes, Rogan said things like that and it creeped me out. I jammed my hands in my jeans pockets lest he ask me to actually hold the invisible furry thing. "I remember last summer, I felt them around just before Cordelia would turn up."

At this statement, Dash whipped his head around. "Keisha, you cannot be near Cordelia." His handsome features pinched, worry lining his eyes.

"I know, I know. Everyone tells me to stay away from the witch, but nobody tells me why. I don't know anyone at Windy Springs who isn't scared of her, so why can't you just get rid of her, if she's such a problem? I mean, you're the boss, right?" Too late, I remembered Rogan telling me that Cordelia was Dash's sister.

"Don't you think I would if I could, lass? She's bound to the forest, unable to leave. Until I can find a way to break that curse, I am burdened with trying to keep our friends at Windy Springs from being hurt by her. The best I can do is ask Juniper to weave a protection spell around those I feel are in danger."

It was frustrating, constantly being told to believe unbelievable things that weren't explained in any satisfactory fashion. "I don't understand."

Dash sighed heavily. "Cordelia and I share a mother, but have different fathers." He dropped into one of the vinyl recliners. Dragged a huge hand across his blue eyes. He looked suddenly older in that instant. "Her father was something… else. Not Knowing. Something evil. Cordelia is both Knowing and like her father. Very powerful. To keep her in check, before his death, her father bound her to the land. The forest. I've been trying for years to find a way to safely break the curse, but it's not easy, because if she's allowed to roam free, and someone out there…" He waved his hand around in the air, "…gets hurt, that's my burden to bear. I need to find a way to both release her from the forest, and keep her away from the rest of the world. Unless… she dies. Then, the worry is over for all of us. God help me, sometimes I wish she would just drop over in her witch's shack, and I'd bury her in the back of the woods and be done with it all."

A chill snaked up my spine. I thought of what they'd done to Vince, working together with their abilities. "Can't you just take care of her? Erase her mind or… ?" I had no idea what all their abilities encompassed, so I trailed off.

"Would that I could, lass. Would that I could. But alas, it doesn't work that way on another of our kind. If she wasn't Knowing, I could. And I *would*. Without a second thought. But she holds the same power as I, plus the power of her father. Believe me, I've tried."

"I think she made me sick when I was pregnant. Sometimes, I would see her, and get the most awful cramps in my stomach." How old was she, anyway? Maybe she would just fall down dead soon. She seemed old. Had to be upwards of sixty-some.

Rogan and Dash locked eyes. "She seems to have a special interest in Evie," Rogan said slowly. "We'll have to be cautious, though Dash has taken what steps he can to keep you both safe."

"Evie? Why would she care anything about my daughter? I don't even really know her." But the thought that she might have some fascination with Evie made my head spin. "And what do you mean, Dash has taken steps to keep us safe?"

Neither of them spoke for a minute, and then Evie began to wiggle around. I went to her crib, unzipping the tent just enough, so I could reach in and touch her. Comfort her. I watched her tiny chest rise and fall, and felt thankful she was breathing much better today.

Finally, Captain Dash spoke, "Juniper has cast a spell of protection around you. Cordelia has to stay ten feet away from you at all times. It's the best I can do." He rubbed his big hands against his head, dragging back the dreads then letting them fall. "As to the other? Cordelia had a child. A daughter. Years ago. She was… taken."

"Taken?" As much as I disliked the woman, my mother-heart clenched at the thought, and I kept my hand on Evie's little arm. To Rogan, I said, "There's a *spell* on me and you didn't say anything about it?" His habit of keeping me in the dark about things was going to be coming to a quick end.

And wait. Juniper, the little round soap lady, could cast spells?

"Shortly after her daughter's disappearance, Cordelia attempted to abduct a little girl. To replace her missing child. She was… distraught, you understand. Used her powers unethically." Dash wagged his head side to side. "It wasn't long after that, she was bound to the forest. To make sure she couldn't do anything like that again. Harm anyone else again."

"The child? Was she hurt?"

"Not the child, no. The mother was injured in the abduction. Again, my sister hasn't been right in her mind since her daughter was taken. She wasn't always this way, see. But we have to keep her from hurting anyone else. The little girl, though, we got her away from Cordelia, eventually. Got her home with her family. The mother recovered. It's been a long time ago, now."

Nausea bubbled up inside me, and I thought maybe that energy drink had been a bad idea. Well, the energy drink coupled with the lack of food, the invisible furry thing and the knowledge about the weird witch that had just been laid on me, plus the news about Evie and her underdeveloped trachea.

Which reminded me, I still needed to explain that to Rogan. That was, of course, unless he already knew. "Rogan," I zipped the tent back up and went to him. "Doctor Towers came while you were sleeping."

He set the mudgen down on Dash's lap and gave me his full attention. "What is it?" His worried expression told me he didn't know.

"Captain Dash? Could you give us a few minutes alone please?"

"Certainly. I should feed him anyway," he said, opening his pants pocket and dumping the mudgen into it. "I'll step down to the cafeteria for a bit."

"Thanks."

He bowed grandly in our direction before exiting the room.

"What is it, sweetheart? Is it serious?"

His wide green eyes were already welling up. I wondered how it worked, how he knew about some things and not others. Like he knew Evie was sick last night, but he didn't know what had caused it.

I took a deep breath and blew it out slowly. "There's this thing called tracheomalacia," I began, surprising myself by pronouncing the word correctly. "And it's what is wrong with our baby."

THE END

Acknowledgements

This book would not have been possible without the help of those who supported and encouraged me along the way. Thank you to John and Olivia, my first readers for In the Presence of Knowing, and to Katie, Joe, Tiffanie, and Susan, my beta readers. Deep appreciation for my editor, formatter, and cover artist, Leanore Elliot.

About The Author

Valarie Savage Kinney is a writer, fiber artist, and Renaissance festival junkie with a wicked caffeine addiction. She resides in Michigan with her husband, four children, and two insane little dogs. She is the author of Just Hold On, Slither, Heckled, and The Secrets of Windy Springs series, as well as short stories in various anthologies.

Made in the USA
San Bernardino, CA
19 May 2019